AS

THE GIRL ON THE BEACH

Also by Velda Johnston

THE GIRL ON THE BEACH

A Novel of Suspense

VELDA JOHNSTON

DODD, MEAD & COMPANY

New York

1 2 3 4 5 6 7 8 9 10

Library of Congress Cataloging-in-Publication Data

Johnston, Velda.
The girl on the beach.

I. Title.
PS3560.0394G57   1987   813'.54   87-15702
ISBN 0-396-09190-3

For Loraine Haynes

AUTHOR'S NOTE: *Blackfish Island and the towns of Camelot and Mockstown are entirely fictitious.*

THE GIRL ON THE BEACH

CHAPTER ONE

Awakening abruptly, she found that the room's air had turned very cold.

Perhaps it was the drop in temperature that had aroused her. More likely, it was the bright moonlight flooding through the uncurtained window to lie in a silver-blue rectangle on the splintery old floor. For a few moments, reluctant to forsake the bed's warmth, inadequate as it was, she lay clutching the blankets close to her chin. Then, throwing them aside, she sat up, thrust her feet into quilted slippers, and lifted her old navy flannel robe from the back of a straight chair.

Knotting the robe's sash around her, she went out into the upstairs hall. She did not turn on the light, lest it wake her so thoroughly that she would not be able to get back to sleep. She opened the door of the linen closet and took down from its shelf one of the wool blankets she had placed there that afternoon, with no idea that she would need extra bed covering so soon. She had not expected North Carolina nights to be this chill, even in March.

Back in the bedroom she spread the blanket over the double bed. Like most of the sparse furnishing in this house, it was old, not enough so to be quaint or charming, just old enough to be rather uncomfortable, with a slight valley running down the middle of its innerspring mattress. She crossed to the window and reached up to pull down the shade. Then, arrested by the night's cold beauty, she let her arm fall to her side.

When she had gone to bed around eight that evening, exhausted by the drive down from New York and the task of carrying her belongings, unassisted, into this house, the moon had been only a cloud-masked glow. Now the clouds were gone except for a few drifting wisps. An almost full moon cast a glittering path over the water. Its light gave a bluish tinge to the foaming waves that washed up onto a narrow strip of wet sand. Nearer by, between the sand and the rectangle of dead grass that served this house as a lawn, was a rock-strewn stretch about twenty feet wide. The rocks, too, glistened under that flood of light.

A question about those rocks came into her still drowsy mind. Had they been deposited here thousands of years ago by a retreating glacier? Probably not. Probably glaciers had never extended as far south as this little island off the midAtlantic coast. But whatever their origin, these strewn rocks must keep this stretch of beach from being really popular, even in midsummer.

Again she reached up to draw the shade. And again she paused, her fingers on the pull ring. There had been movement at the right-hand edge of her vision. Someone was walking along that narrow strip of sand between the low breakers and the wide swathe of rocks. A woman. A young woman, to judge by her slenderness and her lithe walk. Well, that wasn't surprising, even on a night this chill. She herself, if she were not so tired, and if her spirit was not so weighted, might have wanted to wander for a while along that moon-flooded beach.

The woman down there had stopped and turned toward the house. She seemed to be looking up at this second-floor window, although Kate realized that it was highly unlikely that anyone standing on the beach could see into this darkened room. Again Kate felt sure that the girl was young, perhaps half a dozen years younger than herself. Around twenty, say.

What was more, she was unusually attractive. Kate was convinced of it, despite the fifty feet or so that separated them. She had a strong impression of a classic face, wide of forehead and clean-lined of jaw. No way of telling the color of the eyes, but Kate could see that they were wide set. The straight hair a little more than shoulder length looked bluish white, but that of course was a trick of the moonlight. By day it must be pale yellow.

The girl's dress, also of some pale color, was a loose, caftanlike garment. For a moment that puzzled Kate. In her mind, caftans were associated with warm weather. Then she realized that there was no reason why a caftan should not be made of wool rather than gauze.

The girl turned, moved on up the beach. Kate watched her for a few seconds. Then, aware that the cold was striking through her robe and her quilted slippers, and aware too that if she did not get back to sleep soon she might lie awake brooding the rest of the night, she turned and went back to her bed.

CHAPTER
TWO

She had been awake nearly an hour the next morning
before she remembered the episode during the night.

It was a cold morning of wind-polished blue sky and
an even bluer sea, flecked with whitecaps. Gulls wheeled
and plummeted through the chill sunlight. She could hear
their discordant cries as, in a heavy white cotton tee-shirt
and old plaid skirt, she moved about the kitchen, heating
water in a battered but well-polished aluminum tea kettle,
inserting bread slices into an equally old and clean electric
toaster. The whole house seemed to be like that, she
reflected. All the rooms she had walked through yesterday
afternoon and this morning reminded her of Andrew
Wyeth paintings. The same cold light falling through
uncurtained windows into clean, sparsely furnished rooms
that were empty at the moment but not deserted. You felt
that people had withdrawn from that room only a little
while ago, leaving a vibration in the air—

It was at that point in her thoughts that she remembered the young woman on the beach.

Now the whole episode seemed to have a dreamlike
quality. Perhaps it *was* a dream. No, she really had gotten up

sometime during the night and drawn the window shade. This morning the newly risen sun had shone through its small cracks and pinpoint perforations, casting a pattern of dashes and dots on the bare floor. But then, it could be that she had pulled down the shade before she went to bed. It could be that only in a dream had she crossed to the window, and looked out, and seen a girl sauntering through the moonlight—

Stop it, she commanded herself. She was not still a poor, fragmented creature, taking refuge in dreams so vivid that even after she awoke it was the dream that seemed real, not the white-capped nurse bending over her with a paper cup and a pill.

No, she hadn't dreamed the girl. True, it seemed odd that an attractive young woman should be walking alone through the winter moonlight. But compared to the crazy behavior of people she had known, such eccentricity seemed mild indeed. She thought of some of her co-workers at that New York advertising agency. Bright, talented, hellbent on big-success-before-thirty-five, they had ended up blowing it all—jobs, BMW's, Eastside condos—on the white powder they inhaled.

From the cupboard she took down a thick cup and saucer of white crockery and a chipped but rather nice willow-patterned small plate. She spooned instant coffee into the cup, poured hot water over it, put toast on the plate. She started to sit down at the table with its worn red-and-white checked cloth of some plastic material. Then, changing her mind, she carried her breakfast down the short hall, past the newel post of the brown-carpeted stairs, and into the living room. It was a square, medium-sized room, furnished with a fairly new but ugly brown over-

6

stuffed sofa and matching armchair. The threadbare rug, of some sort of floral pattern now faded to a pinkish blur, was too small for the floor space. There was a fireplace, its stone floor swept clean of ashes, its mantel painted dark green.

She would eat on that old card table beside the front window, so that she could look out at the ocean.

She sat down at the table, took a bite of toast, and looked at her paint case and easel. Carrying them from her VW the afternoon before, she had placed them in a corner of this room. This would be her studio, she decided. It not only had a window facing the sea, but one in the north wall, too.

As yet she had no idea of what sort of pictures she would paint. Nor did she have any hope of discovering that she had suddenly turned into a Georgia O'Keefe. Even stretched to its limits, hers would be a small talent. But at least the pictures she painted here would be designed to give her pleasure, and not to sell soap or cigarettes. What was more, finding out how well she could paint would be part of her exploration of the new Kate, the one she hoped would grow strong enough to withstand any additional shocks the future might hold for her.

Near where she had placed her easel, a narrow mirror with a chipped gilt frame hung on the wall. In it she could see her reflected face. It wasn't a face that caused heads to turn, but it was nice enough, the eyes brown and long-lashed, the faintly aquiline nose dusted with pale freckles, the mouth with its full, sensitive-looking underlip. Her brown hair, she noticed, needed cutting. Was there a hairdresser on this island? Probably not. Well, it didn't really matter.

7

She took a sip of coffee and then turned her face to the window.

Again there was someone out there. Not on the narrow strip of sand. That had been covered by the tide. He stood motionless on the rocky part of the beach, a dark-haired man, young or at least youngish, in a heavy dark red shirt and blue jeans.

They stared at each other through the glass. Kate felt a sudden unease. That girl last night. And now this man. Why should either of them be so interested in this house?

For the first time she had a sense of her isolation. The closest neighboring house, a small bungalow, stood about two hundred yards to the south. At this time of the year it probably was unoccupied. To the north there were no houses at all, just the island's end and the entrance to the short causeway stretching to the mainland. She thought of the telephone in the cubbyhole beneath the staircase. The real estate agent, when Kate had last talked to her from New York, had assured her that the phone would be hooked up. Kate assumed that it had been.

The man was still there. She became aware that there was something abstracted as well as intent in his gaze, as if he were seeing something more than the house, something more than herself, seated beside the window.

Then his expression changed, became self-conscious, even embarrassed. He turned, walked a few steps to his right, then halted again and faced the house. Now he wore what apparently was meant to be a reassuring smile. He walked forward.

He was coming to the front door.

She reminded herself that this was not New York, where only a fool would open her door to an unexpected stranger. What was more, everyone knew that islands,

8

especially tiny ones like this, were seldom the scene of serious crimes. An island did not offer a criminal several escape routes after he had committed his misdeed. What was more, the only village on this island, Camelot, couldn't have a year-round population of more than a couple of thousand. A town that small wasn't likely to include a serious felon. Nevertheless, she was glad that some previous tenant—a summer visitor from a big city, perhaps?—had installed a burglar chain on the front door.

She heard his steps on the small front porch, then his knock. She latched the chain before opening the door about eight inches. "Yes?"

He moved to one side, apparently so that she would have a better view of him. He was taller than she had realized, about five feet eleven. Probably it was his broad shoulders and his muscled neck—the neck of an athlete or a man who worked out regularly—that had made her think of him as stocky.

He said, "I could tell you were uneasy."

She didn't answer, just looked at him. His eyes were navy blue under black brows that matched his slightly curling hair. His nose was blunt, his mouth wide, his chin football player square. It was a pleasant enough face, until you noticed something embittered in his gaze and in the set of his mouth.

He said, "Maybe I was wrong, but I thought I ought to tell you that there is nothing to be scared of. I came to take a look at this house only because I used to live here."

"When was that?"

"Twelve years ago."

Twelve years before he must have been around twenty, or perhaps a year or two older. She said, "You mean you grew up in this house?"

9

"No, I grew up in Mockstown, or rather, a few miles outside of it."

Mockstown, she knew, was the town, about four times the size of Camelot, at the other end of the causeway. She had bought groceries and household supplies at the supermarket in Mockstown the afternoon before.

He said, "Do you mind my asking you something? Have you bought this house?"

"No, I rented it through a real estate agent in Camelot. The house, I understand, is owned by a woman named Hillier."

"That's right. Hattie Hillier." He was silent for a moment. As they looked at each other, Kate became aware of something else about him. Embittered loneliness blew from him like a wind. She recognized it because she knew about that kind of loneliness. She'd learned about it during her stay in the hospital.

"Well," he said, "goodbye," and turned away.

"Wait." He turned back. She said, "My name's Kate Kiligrew."

"Mine's Martin Donnerly."

"How did you get here? I mean, is your car up on the road?"

"No. It's in the village. I walked here along the beach."

"It's sort of a cold day for a walk. Perhaps you'd like a cup of coffee before you start back."

She found it hard to decipher the expression that leaped into his face. Obviously the invitation surprised and gratified him. (It had rather surprised her too. She hadn't known she was going to ask him in until she started to do

10

so.) But also he looked strangely reluctant, almost as if he were afraid of something.

Afraid of what? Of himself, of how he might behave? Or was he afraid that she might try to seduce him? Feeling a rush of annoyance, she was about to withdraw her invitation when he said, "Coffee would be just fine, if it's not too much trouble."

"No trouble." She unlatched the chain on the door. "It's instant."

He followed her down the short hall and into the living room. Picking up her cup and saucer from the card table, she turned to look at him. He had stopped just inside the doorway. His gaze was fixed on a brass hook that protruded from the plaster wall a couple of feet above the fireplace mantel. In her tour of the house the day before she hadn't noticed the hook. She wondered what had hung there. A picture? A large mirror?

With the bleakness in his eyes even more pronounced, he turned toward her. Then the expression gave way to a stiffly courteous smile.

"Please sit down," she said, "I'll only be a moment."

In the kitchen she reheated her own coffee and prepared a cup for him. When she came back into the living room, a battered metal tray in her hands, he got to his feet and stood there until she had placed the tray on the table and sat down. He had performed the small courtesy with an unselfconscious ease she would not have expected to find in this out-of-the-way place. It made her wonder about his background.

"Cream? Sugar?"

"Neither, thanks." Looking over her shoulder at the

11

easel leaning against the wall, he took a sip of his coffee and then asked, "Are you an artist?"

"Commercial artist. Advertising agency layouts."

He smiled. "You won't find many ad agencies on Blackfish Island."

"I know. But I already have a job in New York. I'm on—sort of an extended leave."

He didn't ask why she was on leave, or why she had come to this small community, especially at this time of year. But the questions seemed to hover in the air.

She said, "Was your family here with you?"

"My family?"

"When you lived here twelve years ago."

After a long moment he said, "I lived here with my wife."

The words brought her a slight shock. Somehow she had not thought of him as married, or ever having been married.

Did he still have a wife, or had the marriage ended? And if so, how? Had she deserted him, divorced him? Whatever had happened, it still affected him deeply. There was pain and bitterness not only in his eyes, but in his voice.

She searched her mind for a remark that would encourage him to talk and yet not sound intrusive. She could think of nothing.

Coffee cup in hand, he had turned his head to gaze out the window. Now he said, "Look! Blackfish."

Far out, almost to the horizon, a line of about a dozen creatures were arching gracefully into the sunlight and then diving beneath the choppy blue sea. Kate said, "They look more like porpoises than fish."

"They're just called blackfish. They're really a species of small whale. They migrate past here every year. Hence this island's name, I suppose."

He paused, and then went on, "The name of the village used to be Blackfish too, until they changed it to Camelot."

"I know."

His gaze was quizzical. "Someone told you?"

"I suppose so. Anyway, I learned years and years ago that the name had been changed. When I was a little girl I came here two summers in a row with my parents."

"I see."

He waited for her to speak, then set down his cup and looked at the watched strapped to his wrist. It was a well-muscled wrist, even more deeply tanned than his face.

"Thank you for the coffee."

"You're welcome."

"I must leave now. I think I'll go back to the village by the road. Easier on the feet than those rocks."

"Then you'll want to go out the back way."

As he followed her along the hall to the kitchen she became aware that she was wondering what he thought of her appearance. The realization dismayed her. It was the first time since the accident that she had cared whether or not a man found her attractive.

Did it mean that she was getting well emotionally? Or did it mean that she was the same damn fool she had been before she landed in the hospital? While there, she had made a vow that never again would a man be able to hurt her. If and when in the future she formed a relationship with a man, he would be someone who cared for her more deeply than she cared for him, someone who was vulnera-

13

ble to hurt from her rather than the other way around.

But here she was, wondering whether or not this man liked her looks, this stranger of whom she knew almost nothing except that he felt strong emotion for a woman who had been, and perhaps still was, his wife.

Her thoughts made her voice cool when, on the other side of the backdoor screen, he turned to thank her again for the coffee. They exchanged goodbyes. She watched him walk up the path which led past the garage, a small boxy structure which faced, not toward the house, but toward the asphalt road leading to Camelot.

CHAPTER
THREE

She spent the rest of the morning unpacking the second of the two large suitcases she had brought with her and measuring all the windows in the house. She had decided that window curtains would do more than anything else to temper the austerity of these sparsely furnished rooms. An extravagance, yes, but perhaps the real estate agent or the owner would share their cost.

After a tuna sandwich lunch, she wrote a shopping list and then changed into a bulky yellow sweater and slim black skirt. She locked the back door behind her and walked to her gray VW in the garage.

As she drove toward the village she realized that even though she surely had traveled this road with her parents, it had no part in her four-and-five-year-old memories of this island. All of those memories were pleasant. She could recall racing along the red-carpeted corridors of that brand new motel, built by the developers who had persuaded the townspeople to change the name of the little community from Blackfish to Camelot. (Why Camelot? Because of the musical? Or because people had begun to refer to the

Kennedy White House as Camelot?) She had enjoyed splashing in the motel pool, and enjoyed even more running along the wet sand at the ocean's edge, often in pursuit of some small waterfowl. As if sure that their matchstick legs could move faster than her chubby ones, they had never taken flight but just skittered a tantalizing yard or so ahead of her. And she could remember standing at the water's edge while a retreating wave had washed sand from beneath her feet, tickling the soles. She had felt a dizzied sensation, half delightful, half frightening, that everything around her was in motion, not just the sand and the water but the sky. Losing her balance she had plopped to the cold sand, with another spent wave washing around her.

That must have been her first summer on the island, when she was four. Her parents had brought her back here the next summer, but the year after that the three of them had spent two summer weeks with a distant relative in Maine. And by the summer after that, her parents had been divorced, and her father, with his new wife, had gone to the Saudi Arabian job to which his engineering firm had transferred him. He was still in the Middle East, making only rare visits to the United States. Kate had seen him three times in the twenty years since the divorce.

The older she grew, the more Kate admired the way her mother had behaved after the divorce. She had not taken to alcohol or to overeating. Despite the generous divorce settlement, which included an East Eightieth Street condo, she had gone back to the Wall Street firm which had employed her before her marriage. She had become neither promiscuous nor a man hater. She dated, and although none of her dates stayed at the apartment

16

overnight, Kate suspected that some of her mother's out-of-town weekends had been spent, not with "friends," but one particular friend.

Most praiseworthy of all, Kate felt, had been her mother's attitude toward her only child. Although she must have been tempted to lavish emotion on her small daughter, she had treated Kate much as she had before, lovingly, but with a certain humorous detachment. Thus Kate, unlike the only offspring of so many widowed or divorced women, had never been burdened with a guilty sense that she must make up for the husband and the other children that her mother lacked.

When Kate was nineteen, her mother had died, thrown to a Central Park bridle path by a mount that had shied at something or other, whether a blowing newspaper or unleashed dog no one had ever known. Her neck had snapped, killing her instantly. Despite her numbing grief, Kate was aware that her mother had died much as she would have wanted to—impeccably groomed, clad in well-cut jodphurs, and with a riding crop still clutched in her slender hand.

Then a sophomore at the Gotham School of Fine Arts, Kate had thought she would have to leave college, take a job, and perhaps sell the apartment. Then she learned just how successful her mother had been. There was enough money to enable Kate to hold onto the condo and finish school. Within days after her graduation, she was hired by one of the oldest New York advertising agencies.

Now she had entered the little town which, almost a quarter of a century ago, had renamed itself, no doubt with hopes of a soaring prosperity fed by hordes of summer visitors. It was plain that those hopes had not been

17

fulfilled. Many of the shops along the main street had for rent signs in their windows. The movie theater's marquee announced that it was "Open Sat. & Sun." When she reached the only part of town she remembered, the Camelot Motel, she saw that it had been turned into a shopping mall. The pool in which she had learned to swim, with her father's hand supporting her round little belly, had been paved over to provide additional parking space. Not that space seemed scarce, at least not at the moment. Most of the rectangles, outlined with white paint on the cement, stood empty. Many of the former motel units, their pink plaster facades replaced by plate glass, also were empty. For the rest, the mall offered the services of a drugstore, paint store, five-and-dime, a dry cleaner, and the Kelso Real Estate Agency. It was with a Leora Kelso that she had arranged to rent the house at the other end of the island. Later she would call on Mrs. Kelso. But first she must open an account at the local bank.

She left the mall by its far exit, drove back along the wide main street, and stopped before the red brick First Merchants' Bank and Trust. (Why was it, Kate wondered, that you never saw a Second Merchants' Bank and Trust?) Inside the bank she found that business was slow there, too. Two women, both thin, both with the shapes of hair curlers showing through the scarves knotted under their chins, stood at one of the tall desks, filling out some sort of forms. In one of the grilled tellers' cages a middle-aged man was counting out bills for a customer, an elderly man in overalls. Near the entrance, the railed enclosure where bank officials conferred with customers was entirely empty. Kate waited until the overalled man turned away, thrusting a thin sheaf of bills into a worn wallet, and then walked over to the teller.

"I'd like to open an account, please."

He looked at her curiously through rimless glasses. "Miss Weyant will help you." He nodded toward the railed enclosure. "That first desk is hers. Just take a seat."

The first desk bore a nameplate: "Miss Vanessa Weyant, Vice President." There must have been some sort of intercom because less than a minute after Kate had taken the customer's chair a door in the wall opened and a woman walked toward the desk. Kate felt surprise. The term "vice president" had suggested to her a severely plain spinster, middle-aged or older. This woman looked to be several years under forty. And she was good-looking, with dark hair cut and shaped into a sleek cap, clear gray eyes, and a clean-featured face marred only by a somewhat heavy jaw line. Her clothing—gray jacket, paisley skirt, white shirt with a little black string tie—might have been worn by one of those dressed-for-success women you see toting brief-cases in and out of Wall Street offices. Where did she buy such clothes? Not in Camelot, surely. Perhaps she patronized the better mail order houses, or made shopping trips to Raleigh or Richmond.

"Good afternoon." The woman sat down. "My name's Vanessa Weyant." She added wryly, "And if you're wondering how I got to be a vice president, it was through hard work and the fact that my father owns the bank."

Kate smiled appreciatively. "I'm Kate Kiligrew."

"Are you the one who rented the Hillier house?"

"Yes."

Vanessa Weyant had been sure that was the case. Off-season visitors, especially ones who opened bank accounts, were rare.

She studied the girl to whom Leora Kelso, sly one that she was, had rented that perennial lemon, the Hillier

19

house. This Kate Kiligrew was attractive. Intelligent, too, to judge by her voice and facial expression. Not happy, though. The brown eyes had a shadowed look. Running away from something, then. But why run to Blackfish Island, of all places?

Kate reached into her shoulder bag and then laid a certified check for ten thousand dollars on the desk. When she withdrew the money from her New York bank she knew that it probably would be more than sufficient for her needs. But after all, she wasn't sure how long she would be down here.

"You want to place all of this in checking?"

"Yes, please."

Vanessa Weyant took forms from a drawer, laid them on the desk, handed Kate a ballpoint pen. Head bent, Kate filled in the blanks and then extended the forms to the other woman.

Vanessa Weyant looked swiftly through them. "Everything seems in order. But I'm afraid you can't draw against this during the next three days. A bank rule. A self-serving one, of course. We can make a little money loaning out your ten thousand for the next few days. You know, the float. It won't be much, but with a bank this small every little bit helps."

"Yes, I've heard of the float." Kate wondered about a certain quality in Vanessa Weyant, a kind of dry self-mockery. "I have enough cash to last me for three days."

"Good. Tell me, is this your first visit to Camelot?"

"No, my parents brought me here for two summers in a row when I was a small child."

"That must have been about the time that the town decided to take a new name and change itself into another Hilton Head."

20

Kate nodded and then asked, "What happened?"

"Happened?"

"Why didn't it work? Why did the motel where we stayed become a shopping mall? A not very successful one, I'd say."

Vanessa shrugged. "Lots of reasons. Our damned rocky beaches, for one thing. There are only a few places where the beach is sandy above the high water mark. Too, the new motel set its rates too low in hope of attracting a large clientele. Then they compounded the error by buying up lots of land, in the hope that summer visitors would build their own cottages here. That didn't work out. Then there's the causeway. It's in terrible shape, as you must have noticed. It always has been. The town hoped the county would fix it, but they never did.

"Anyway, when the developers went under they took quite a few people's savings with them. Even this bank had invested money." She smiled. "But that was twenty years ago. Your ten thousand is quite safe."

"I'm sure it is."

"If there's any way I can help you while you're here—"

"Thank you." Kate hesitated and then said, "There is one thing you could tell me right now. Do you know a Martin Donnerly?"

Vanessa's long-fingered hands, holding the forms Kate had filled out, grew very still. "Why do you ask?"

"I met him this morning. He came to the house—said he used to live there—and I asked him in for a cup of coffee. I thought you might know him."

Vanessa thought, know him! Martin was by far the most important person in her life. Some might think it was because of her father that she stayed on in this tiny town

21

where there were no single men she would consider marrying. But Martin Donnerly was the real reason. She had been sure he would come back someday. And when he did, he would realize that she was the one he should have married, all those years ago. He'd realize that at most, he should never have felt more than a passing letch for that bitch, Donna Sue.

With her cold, clear insight, Vanessa Weyant knew that what she felt for Martin Donnerly was obsession. She had recognized it as that for years now, ever since that summer when she was twenty-four and he was eighteen. The difference in their ages hadn't mattered. Nothing had mattered, nor did it now.

He *had* come back, earlier that month. A week ago, overriding her father's objections, she had granted him a bank loan, so that he could realize that old dream of his of building a boatyard on the western side of the island. All that week, under her cool, business-like exterior, she had felt a feverish joy.

But now here was this girl. Not just any girl, but an attractive one with an air of quiet good breeding. A commercial artist, according to the forms she had filled out. She must be a good one. The firm she worked for was among the most prestigious in the country.

Maybe there was no danger. Just the same, best to nip the whole thing in the bud.

Kate felt puzzled. Had she said something wrong? Why was the woman across the desk looking at her like that? "He told me he grew up on the mainland, in Mockstown or near there. Still, I thought you probably knew him."

"He grew up three miles from Mockstown."

22

Vanessa thought of the Donnerly house. Red brick, soaring white columns, a graveled circular drive on the wide lawn. Vanessa knew that a part of Martin's appeal, a very small part, was to her snobbery. The Donnerlys, once highly successful tobacco planters, were the nearest thing to pre-Civil War aristocracy for miles around.

Why, Kate wondered, had the woman's voice been so cold and stiff? Kate said, "At first he rather frightened me, standing there on the beach and staring at the house. But then he came to the door and told me he'd once lived there. I decided he was all right, and so I asked him in for coffee. He seemed quite nice."

Best to let her have it, Vanessa decided. Right smack in the face.

"Yes, he's very nice, if you like killers."

Kate sat motionless. After a moment she gave a forced smile. "I'm afraid I don't get it."

"There's nothing to get, except what I told you. Martin Donnerly is fresh out of the state penitentiary, on parole. He served twelve years of a ten-to-twenty year sentence for second-degree murder."

After a moment Kate managed to ask, "Who did he—"

"He killed his wife. With a shotgun, in that house."

Kate felt nausea in the pit of her stomach. A few hours ago she had sat drinking coffee with a murderer. Maybe he had killed his wife in that very room.

"It seems hard to believe. Did he ever admit—"

"No. But how many murderers do confess? Twelve good men and true—or rather, seven women and five men—found that he did do it, and that's what counts.

"Now don't look so worried," she went on. "I doubt if he'll come there again. But just to make sure, you might

23

tell our chief of police about it. He'll warn Martin to stay away from you."

And that, Vanessa thought, should take care of *that*. Martin would never forgive this New York girl for his humiliation.

"Thank you. Perhaps I will go to the chief of police."

Vanessa Weyant took from a desk drawer a folding checkbook with a cover of bright yellow and handed it across the desk. When Kate stood up she found that her legs felt rather weak.

"Goodbye, Miss Weyant. And thank you."

CHAPTER
FOUR

Out in the cool sunlight she drove about fifty yards and then stopped at the curb in front of the Bluebell Lunchroom. What should she do, pack up and go back to New York? Back to all those memory laden places she was not yet able to face? Restaurants and theaters to which Richard had taken her. That infants' wear shop on upper Madison Avenue, where she had stood looking dreamily at a window filled with christening gowns and tiny knitted jackets.

No, she wouldn't go back to New York just yet.

Where, then? Someplace further south? This time of year such places would still be crowded with refugees from the northern winter. Besides, it had taken her such a long time, lying in the hospital, to decide upon this place.

But if she stayed on here in that isolated house, shouldn't she have some protection besides locks on the front and back doors? A dog, perhaps? But no. Dogs were banned by her New York condominium. She could not take in an animal for a few weeks or months, earn its love and trust, and then return it to some pound or kennel.

Perhaps she should follow Vanessa Weyant's suggestion and go to the chief of police. Since Martin Donnerly was on parole, surely he would not defy an official order to leave her alone.

Anyway, now that she had thought it over, she felt that he would not choose to return. He would know that it would not be long before someone would tell her where he had spent the last twelve years and why. He would realize how unwelcome another sight of him would be.

But wasn't she crediting him with a sensitivity he might not possess? After all, a man who had shot his wife to death—

In cold blood? Probably not. Otherwise it would have been first-degree murder, not second. Perhaps there were extenuating circumstances.

Don't decide now, she told herself. Best to see the real estate agent, just as she had planned. Still feeling shaken, she drove to the shopping mall and stopped in front of the Kelso Real Estate Agency. Beyond the plate glass a plump woman with short gray curls all over her head sat at a desk. Leora Kelso herself? Kate was almost sure of it. When they talked over the phone she had thought the woman had a plump-sounding voice.

Kate walked in. "Mrs. Kelso?"

"Miss Kelso." Her small blue eyes were bright behind black-rimmed harlequin glasses. "And you're Miss Kiligrew, right?"

"Yes." Winter visitors must indeed be rare if Leora Kelso had known instantly who she was.

"Sit down, sit down."

When Kate had taken the straight chair at one end of the desk, Miss Kelso asked, "How do you like your house?"

26

"It's very clean," Kate said, somewhat evasively. "But I wanted to ask you. Is it all right to use the fireplace?"

"Heavens, no! Didn't I mention that on the phone? Miss Hillier—she's the elderly lady who owns it—had the chimney blocked off twenty years ago, when she put in the furnace. Try to use the fireplace and you'll burn the house down, sure." She paused. "Anything else?"

"The place is—somewhat underfurnished."

"Now look. I could have put you in one of the summer cottages I handle. But all they've got is little gas heaters. Besides, you said you were an artist and wanted a quiet place with lots of light."

Leora Kelso had had still another reason for wanting the girl to take that particular house. Miss Hillier in recent years had been complaining about the low revenue from her property. True, a few times some family had stayed for a whole summer. But some tenants had left even before their first month's rent was up, often with no more excuse than that they didn't find the place "comfortable."

"The house *is* clean and light, isn't it?" Miss Kelso persisted.

"Yes." Particularly without window curtains, Kate added mentally.

"If there are some small things you wanted, kitchen equipment, say—"

"No, I can get by with what's there. But I would like to put up curtains. I've measured quite a few of the windows."

"You'll take the curtains with you when you leave?"

"No, they wouldn't fit my apartment windows."

Leora felt distinctly annoyed. Early last summer a couple had rented the house for a month and then, after

27

three weeks, had decided to leave. When she wouldn't refund any of the rent, they had retaliated by taking the curtains with them.

"Let's do it this way. You put up the curtains, and when you're ready to leave, I'll pay you half their cost." Not a bad deal, Leora reflected. She herself would have had to put up curtains sooner or later, either paying for them herself or getting the money out of Miss Hillier, which would be considerably harder than getting it out of Fort Knox.

"All right."

"Anything else I can do for you?"

Kate hesitated. "Perhaps you could give me some information. I've just come from the bank. Miss Weyant there said there'd been a murder in the house I rented."

Leora felt annoyed. Why had Vanessa told the girl that? It wasn't like her to be loose-tongued. "Yes, there was a murder. It never occurred to me to mention it to you. It happened years ago. Lots of people have lived there since."

"Did you—did you know the woman who was killed?"

"Donna Sue? Everybody knew Donna Sue."

"What was she like?"

"White trash."

Kate felt a little shocked. It was the first time she had actually heard anyone use that term.

"All the Welkers are white trash," Leora went on. "Their place is over in the pine woods beyond Mockstown. Old Roy Welker hunts and traps and now and then does a little moonshining. All three of the boys were in and out of trouble with the law since they were grammar school age. As for the girls, Donna Sue and her twin—" She broke off, snapped her fingers. "Darleen Mae, that's her name. Darleen Mae."

"You say they were twins?"

"Yes. Darleen Mae was born second. Something went wrong. Anyway, she's never been right in the head. As for Donna Sue, she'd been sidling up to anything in pants since before she was twelve years old."

Kate said, after a moment, "It's so hard to imagine a man like Martin Donnerly—"

"You *know* him?"

"We met. I mentioned him to Miss Weyant. Then she told me about the murder."

So that was it. Vanessa had wanted to make sure that this good-looking New York girl steered clear of Martin. Poor Vanessa. She thought she was so smooth, so superior to the other people in this town. She didn't realize that they could read her like a book, at least where Martin Donnerly was concerned. And if she thought she could convince people that the bank was financing Martin's boatyard just as a business deal, she had another think coming.

Kate said, "I talked to him for only a few minutes. Still, I find it hard to imagine him marrying a girl like that."

"That's because you didn't know Donna Sue. She was gorgeous enough to make almost any man lose his head. And Martin was only twenty-one or so, fresh out of engineering college."

"Does anyone know why—"

"Why he killed her? Not for sure. He never gave any reason, just kept denying he'd done it. But we all knew she'd given him plenty of provocation."

She paused. "Not to change the subject," she said, changing it, "but I don't suppose you've hired a cleaning woman yet."

"I didn't plan to."

"Myrtle Thompson is awfully good." Myrtle was a cousin of Leora's, and paid her ten percent of whatever she earned cleaning for Leora's tenants. "You might not think it, but a lot of sand blows into those beach houses. And if you want to paint, instead of sweeping and scrubbing—"

Kate hesitated. It was true that sometimes, reluctant to tackle a painting, she found herself spending a disproportionate amount of time on household tasks.

"She works cheap," Leora said. "Five dollars an hour."

By New York standards, that was indeed cheap. "All right."

"I'll send Myrtle by, so you can arrange what days and so on. Anything else I can do?"

"Is there some kind of town hall here?"

"Oh, sure. You must have passed it. It's that old red brick building a couple of doors from the bank. Mayor's office, chief of police, the works."

"Thank you." Kate stood up. "Goodbye for now."

CHAPTER
FIVE

As she drove down the main street with its many store-for-rent signs, she suddenly wondered why her father had ever chosen this little island as a vacation spot. Then she realized that she knew the probable answer. When Kate was fifteen, her mother told her that for several years before the divorce her father had been partially supporting the woman, a not-too-successful model, who became his second wife. No wonder he had found it expedient to bring his wife and child to a resort motel which had set its prices unusually low.

That must be the town hall up ahead, that red brick building with the American flag flying from its roof. Aware that the sky had begun to cloud over, she parked her car, went inside the building and walked down a short corridor. The doors on either side, were labeled "John Clemson, Mayor," "Julian Charles, Town Clerk," and "Melvin Bosley, Chief of Police."

She opened the door and went in. A freckled youth who looked tall even sitting down lifted his gaze from an old upright typewriter.

31

Kate said, "May I see Chief Bosley?"

"Sure." He stood up, walked leisurely to the door of the inner office, went inside. When he emerged a minute or so later he said, "Chief'll see you."

She walked past the youth and heard him close the door behind her. Melvin Bosley was standing behind his desk.

Perhaps Kate had seen too many movies and TV shows featuring small town police chiefs whose bellies bulged over their belts. Anyway, she had expected Bosley to look like that. Instead he was as tall as his deputy and very thin, with a prominent Adam's apple showing above the open neck of his khaki shirt. His dark eyes were deepset under prominent brow ridges. Despite the ungrayed blackness of his hair, she judged him to be in his late fifties.

"Chief Bosley?"

"That's right."

"My name is Kate Kiligrew. I've rented a house on the northern end of the island."

He nodded. "I heard Leora had rented the Hillier place to someone from New York. Well, sit down, little lady, sit down."

They both sat down, she in a straight chair, he in the creaking swivel chair behind his desk.

"I suppose you know a man named Martin Donnerly."

After a moment he said, "Ought to. I helped send him up. He been bothering you?"

Something had leaped into the dark eyes, a fierce, anticipatory shine. It made Kate wish she hadn't come here.

"Not really. In fact, he seemed quite nice."

"But then you heard he'd murdered his wife, eh, and then he didn't seem so nice."

Donna Sue had been dead for a dozen years now, and yet the chief felt anger whenever he thought of her. Little bitch, putting out for half the men in the county, and yet turning her nose up at him. Him, Melvin Bosley, who'd been an important man in this town since before she was born. Plenty of women had said yes to him, and not all of them because they were afraid not to, for one reason or another. But that little tease, Donna Sue, had always managed to slip away from him.

Well, she'd gotten what was coming to her. Her and that college boy husband of hers both. Not that he looked like a college boy now. He looked like a man who'd done twelve years hard time.

Bosley asked, "What did Martin do? Show up at the place you rented?"

"Yes. After he told me he used to live there, I asked him in for a cup of coffee."

A cup of coffee! A paroled convict, and yet he got asked by a classy-looking dish like this one to have some coffee.

"But now you want to be sure he doesn't come back. Rest easy. I know where he's staying. With his brother at the old Donnerly place on the mainland. I'll phone him and say that if he comes near you I'll report him to his parole officer in Mockstown."

"No, please!" She shrank at the thought of how humiliated Martin Donnerly might feel, forced to take orders from this hate-filled man. She could sense the hate in the air of this little office, although whether it was directed at Martin Donnerly, or at his dead wife, or at the world in general, she could not be sure.

"If I feel I need protection, I—I'll ask you." She paused and then asked, "Is it certain that he—"

33

"Shot his wife? He said he didn't, of course. Said he came home and found her on the floor, full of pellets from the shotgun that always hung above the fireplace. Found the place all torn up, he said, like somebody had been looking for something. But of course he must have emptied out those drawers and ripped up those pillows and so on himself. There were no fingerprints on the shotgun except his, and no fingerprints except his and Donna Sue's anywhere in the house. What's more, there were scratches on his face, and bits of his skin under her fingernails. Oh, yes, he killed her."

Chief Bosley paused. "You ought to at least make sure about the locks on that house. Jed Phillips, runs the hardware store, he's a pretty good locksmith. He'd drop everything and do the job right away if I asked. Suppose I come out to your place this evening and take a look at the doors and windows."

A real classy girl, he was thinking. The cool, smooth kind who made you wonder how quick they'd stop being cool if you could get them between the sheets. And maybe you could. She might not be as out of reach as she looked. After all, a New York girl, some kind of artist, coming down here to stay all by herself—

"Thank you," she said, "but I don't think that will be necessary. If I change my mind, I'll phone you."

She stood up. "Goodbye, Chief Bosley. And thank you again."

CHAPTER
SIX

By the time she left the town hall the sky had clouded over completely. And by the time she finished her shopping at the Camelot Variety Store—hundred-watt bulbs to replace the thriftily dim ones in the house, a fluffy blue mat for the bathroom's linoleum-covered floor, drip-dry curtains for the windows—a light rain had begun to fall. In the grocery store she bought supplies to supplement the ones she had bought in Mockstown the day before. Then she drove the rest of the way through town and started along the road to the house.

She had driven perhaps half a mile along the worn asphalt, bordered on either side by sandy earth dotted with twisted dwarf pines and clumps of bayberry, when the rangy gray cat, a tom to judge by the size of him, darted across the VW's path. Her foot hit the brake pedal. The little car fishtailed across the wet asphalt and then stalled, nose pointed at an angle across the road.

There had been no danger. There wasn't another car in sight. And yet the skidding sensation had brought back a memory so terrible that for perhaps a minute she sat there with her arms crossed on the wheel and her head bowed, fighting nausea. Even after she was able to straighten up and restart the car she felt too shaken to drive. She parked at the roadside and stared through the raindrops trailing down the windshield.

The rain falling on that Connecticut highway that afternoon last January had been heavier than this rain. And Richard had been driving his Porsche fast, far too fast and recklessly for a supposedly happy young man, taking his fiancée—his pregnant fiancée—home to meet his father and mother.

Such behavior was not like Richard Sedge. He never carried anything to reckless extremes. As a successful young stockbroker he worked from nine to five, rather than almost around the clock like some of his feverishly ambitious colleagues. He was prudent even in small matters. He always paid his credit card bills promptly, thus avoiding interest charges. He usually had a drink before dinner, and, if offered a toke at a party, often accepted. Otherwise he steered clear of drugs.

And he was dependable. In the more than a year of their relationship, she had never known him to break his word, either to her or anyone else. It was impossible to imagine him walking out on a wife and child, as her father had. Richard was a good-looking man, tall and thin with a warm smile, but it was that dependable quality of his that had caused her to fall in love. It was something she had sensed in him from almost the first time they met, at a cocktail party given by a woman in her advertising agency.

Until she fell in love, she hadn't really been aware that as a child and adolescent she had felt emotionally deprived. First there had been her father's defection. And after that her mother, too, had been away from her much of the time, in her office during the day, and in the evenings often going out. Although the mature Kate was glad that her mother had not turned to her for all her emotional sustenance, the child Kate had wanted more of her mother's time and attention. She had memories of her six-and-seven-year-old self sitting before the TV set in the afternoon, watching one of those family situation comedies about a father and a mother and three children. She had not been alone. Always she was aware of Carol, the live-in maid, moving about somewhere in the apartment. But as she watched the figures on the little screen she had been aware of a vague emotion she thought of as "feeling bad." It was only after she grew up that she recognized that emotion as loneliness.

With Richard she no longer felt lonely. And as much as she enjoyed their lives together—the dinners, the skiing weekends, the hours of love-making in her apartment or in Richard's smaller but much newer one near Lincoln Center—she felt that the future would hold even more for them. Neither of them had mentioned marriage, but she was sure they would marry before long. And thanks to Richard's high earning ability, plus the money she had inherited from her mother, she could, if she chose, stay home with their offspring for a few years. Smiling a little at the notion, she thought of how the Richard Sedges would be a throwback to those TV families of the sixties and earlier.

The trouble was that before they got around to discussing marriage, she found that she was pregnant.

The discovery first brought her dismay, then excited anticipation, then a certain unease. She never doubted for

37

a moment that Richard would suggest marriage as soon as she told him. And yet he must have had some reason, in that logical mind of his, for not proposing before this that they marry.

For almost two weeks she didn't tell him, held silent by that faint unease and by the guilty knowledge that the pregnancy was her fault. After all, she had assumed the responsibility for preventing such an occurrence. Finally she did tell him one night when they were having dinner in her apartment.

They sat beside the fireplace, with a small silver and china laden table between them. Before she had said more than a few words she saw him stiffen. Only a moment before his face, tanned from the ski slopes, had looked attractively flushed in the light from the dancing flames. Now it took on a muddy hue. He laid his knife and fork carefully on his plate.

Kate's voice faltered into silence.

He asked, "You're sure?"

"Oh, yes. I'm more than two months pregnant."

After a long moment he said, "I don't suppose you would consider—"

"No." Kate's hands had turned cold. "No, I wouldn't."

Again there was silence except for the fire's crackle. "Then I suppose," he said, "that we had better get married as soon as possible."

He was smiling, but it was a forced smile.

Yes, she had been right. She could depend upon Richard. But why, she wondered bleakly, had she been so sure that he would not mind getting married right away? For that matter, why had she been sure that he intended to marry her at any time? True, he had often said that he loved her. But that did not necessarily mean that he planned to spend a lifetime with her.

She forced the words out. "You don't have to marry me, you know."

"Kate, that's just silly. If you insist upon having this child, we must marry."

Must marry.

Where, she wondered, was her pride? Why didn't she get to her feet, make a dignified little speech, and then bid him goodbye? Perhaps it was the new life within her, a life with its own needs, which made her pride seem relatively unimportant.

"We'd better drive up to see my parents right away, and get married before the week's out." Again that forced smile. "After all, there is a limit to just how premature a premature baby can be."

His parents. Could they be the reason he had never asked her to marry him, perhaps never intended to ask her? She had known that the Sedges were old Boston aristocracy, whereas no one in her family had ever been listed in the Social Register. But that had seemed to her of no consequence whatever. She was presentable, intelligent, and successful. What was more, she had grown up attending the right schools and summer camps. So where was the gap?

But perhaps there had been a gap. Perhaps he had grown up knowing that he was expected to marry a Saltonstall or a Lodge. And although part of him must have regarded such restrictions as absurd and out of date, perhaps another part of him—the conservative, firmly sensible part—had felt that his life and his career would proceed more smoothly if he made the sort of marriage expected of him.

She said, "Must we see your parents ahead of time? Couldn't we just—"

"No, Kate." His voice was firm. "They'll be upset enough learning that the marriage is to be so soon. I couldn't just confront them with a *fait accompli*."

Kate had assumed that he had talked of her during the occasional weekends he spent with his parents. Now she wondered if they even knew of her existence.

He looked at his watch. "I'd better telephone them during the next hour or so."

Neither Kate nor Richard had any appetite for the rest of their chicken-curry dinner. They drank coffee. Now matter-of-fact, even cheerful, Richard talked of what they should tell his parents. ("Better to make it the truth. They'll guess it anyway.") Around nine he left to make the phone call from his own apartment.

For a long time that night she lay awake, staring into the dark. As countless women in the same situation have done, she tried to take the optimistic view. The first few months of this enforced marriage might be rough. But when the baby was born Richard would love it. So would the baby's grandparents. Soon she and Richard would be happier together than they had ever been.

And if it did not work out like that? Then she would give him his freedom, and start raising their child alone. Worse things than that could happen to a child. After all, she herself hadn't turned out too badly.

They started up to Boston the next Saturday. Because the Porsche had somehow acquired a flat tire while standing in the public garage, they left Manhattan late. Then on the Throg's Neck Bridge they had been caught in a massive traffic jam behind a jacknifed tractor-trailer truck. Thus it was already early afternoon when they entered Connecticut with its broad highway leading north between winter-brown fields and rolling hills.

While waiting out the traffic jam they had talked about what furniture they would move from Richard's apartment to Kate's larger one. Once they were off the bridge, though, Richard tuned the radio to a pop-rock station and raised the volume high enough that conversation became difficult.

He drove fast, faster than she had ever known him to drive. Once, raising her voice above the music, she suggested that he slow down. "It's starting to rain," she pointed out.

"If I don't drive fast, we won't get there for dinner on time. Mother hates unpunctuality, especially at meals."

Yes, Kate reflected, it was important not to be late. His parents, Richard had said, had seemed to take the news very well, after the initial shock. They had sent warm, welcoming messages to Kate. Nevertheless, it was essential this first meeting go smoothly. A late arrival would be held against *her,* she felt, even though it would be no more her fault than Richard's.

Ten miles north of Hartford they rounded a curve. Ahead was a stalled car. Richard hit the brakes. The Porsche slewed, skidded around until it was pointed in the opposite direction. Struck by an oncoming car, it crashed onto its right side.

When Kate awoke in a Hartford hospital early the next morning, she did not remember the actual crash. Post-trauma amnesia had deprived her of memory of everything that had happened after that first sickening skid.

She had a concussion, they told her, and five broken ribs, and almost certainly some internal injuries. When she asked about Richard, they said that his condition was far less serious. He was being held for observation, though. They gave her a pill, and told her to try to sleep.

It was not until mid-afternoon that they told her she was no longer pregnant.

Richard came into her room about four-thirty and sat down beside her bed. The ruddy light of a winter sunset shone through the window onto his distressed face. There were strips of adhesive tape above his right eye and on his chin. His right wrist was bandaged.

"Darling, how do you feel?"

She heard her own blurred voice. "Not too bad. How about you?"

"A few cuts and sprains. Otherwise I'm okay."

"Did they tell you?" Beneath her heavy sedation, grief stirred. "I'm not going to have that baby."

After a moment he said, "Oh, Kate! I'm sorry."

But she had seen the swift leap of relief in his eyes. She said, "No, you're not sorry. You're glad."

"Kate! What a hell of a thing to say. Of course I'm sorry, sorry about the whole thing. But in a way, maybe it's all to the good. It takes the pressure off. We'll still get married, but not in such a rush."

Yes, now there would be time for the proper announcements in the papers, the proper parties where she would be introduced to all the Sedges and their friends. And if she did her best to charm them, they might find her quite acceptable.

"No," she said.

"No what?"

"We won't get married."

"Now, Kate! This doesn't change things between you and me. I asked you to marry me, and my word still stands."

"I'm giving you back your word. Please go."

"Kate! You don't know what you're saying. You're in no condition to decide such—"

"Go away!" Her voice rose. "Leave me alone."

A nurse came swiftly into the room. "You'd better leave, sir. The patient mustn't be upset."

He stood up. "Very well." His tone was reluctant and his expression distressed. But Kate still could sense his relief.

He went out. The louvered door closed with a sighing sound. The nurse, a middle-aged one with an I've-seen-everything face, didn't ask what the trouble had been. She just gave Kate a pill.

The next day a large basket of yellow roses arrived. With it was a note:

I'll be staying with my parents for the next three days. Their phone is Monument 7-5240. Please let me know as soon as you want to see me again.

Love,

Richard.

So the ball was in her court. She did not hit it back to him.

Four days later she was transferred to a Manhattan hospital not far from her apartment. A couple of times

43

during her three weeks' stay there, a friendly nurse's aide told her that a Mr. Sedge had phoned. No, he hadn't asked to speak to her. He had just asked how she was progressing.

Well, she had never thought of Richard as a man without conscience. Of course he had a conscience, a very upright one, and now it was bothering him. In a way it should not have. By offering her marriage, he had behaved more than honorably. As for the car accident, it had been just that, an accident.

Or had it been? Often she thought of Richard, set-faced, driving at close to eighty while an old Chuck Berry number almost seemed to rock the sports car. Could he have been wishing that something would happen to let him off the hook?

Of course he might have been. But that didn't mean that he would risk maiming or killing himself and her. Unless, perhaps, subconsciously—

She tried to banish the idea, but it kept coming back, sometimes in the form of a bad dream. Richard behind the wheel of a speeding car, his face murderous, intent, while she vainly screamed at him and shook his arm.

The hospital finally released her into the slush and raw air of a Manhattan February. Her ribs were mended and her internal injuries healed. Nevertheless, she spent several days in her apartment before reporting to her office.

Her work did not go well. Perhaps the bad dreams and the resultant broken sleep were to blame. Whatever the reason, two of the layouts she prepared were disapproved. Finally the head of her department called her in. Perhaps she needed more time to recover, he said. Perhaps she should go away someplace for a month or even longer. Her job would be waiting for her when she got back.

But go where? Some ski resort, with people shouting at each other on the slopes and, in the evenings, singing loudly in the firelit lounge? Some even noisier cruise ship, with mountains of food being served every few hours, and passengers in funny hats throwing paper streamers at each other? Neither prospect appealed to her.

If only she had some relative with whom she could stay for a while. But there was no one. From rather shamefaced things her father had said when he was last in New York, she knew it would not do to turn up at his house in Riyadh. His present marriage wasn't going well, despite the fact that he and his wife had three children. The second Mrs. Kiligrew, Kate gathered, would not welcome a visit from the daughter of the first. Her only other relative was a cousin in Oregon, more precisely a cousin of her mother's. Kate hadn't seen her since she herself was ten and the cousin in her late thirties.

But surely there must be someplace she would like to go to, a quiet place where she could paint, not to sell products but to please herself, and then perhaps come back to New York with her emotional wounds healed as well as her bodily ones.

It was then that she thought of Camelot, that place she remembered from her fourth and fifth summers. In those fragmentary memories she had been happy as only a child can be who has a sense, however illusory, of being surrounded by unfailing protection and love.

The temperature ought to be just right in March. Too cool to attract summer people and yet warmer than still frigid New York.

45

The next morning she asked Information if there was a telephone listing for a chamber of commerce in Camelot, North Carolina. No, Information said, there was not. How about a merchants association? Yes, Camelot had one of those.

A few minutes later Kate was talking to a Leora Kelso, real estate agent. Yes, the woman said, she had just the house for an artist. Quiet, with lots of light. Nothing fancy, mind you, but warm and snug with an oil furnace, and very cheap this time of year. And everything furnished except linen and blankets. If Miss Kiligrew would send her a deposit—

Four days later, with two big suitcases, her painting gear, and a flat cardboard chest filled with sheets and blankets, Kate started south. On Blackfish Island, late that afternoon, she found the house immediately. It would be the first house to her left after she crossed the causeway, Leora Kelso had said. She also found the house keys where the real estate agent had said she would leave them, under an upturned bushel basket in one corner of the garage.

Now she raised her head from her crossed arms. The brief rainstorm had blown over, although drops still lingered on the windshield. In the west the sun shone in a rapidly clearing sky. She started the VW and drove toward her rented house.

CHAPTER
SEVEN

She entered the house by the back door, left the packaged curtains and her other variety store purchases on the sinkboard, and put the groceries away in the cupboards and the surprisingly modern refrigerator. Then she went down the hall to the living room. She halted on the threshold, her gaze going to that hook above the fireplace which once had supported a shotgun.

More than likely, Donna Sue had died in this room. But it could have been some other room in this house. Besides, since that violent event of a dozen years ago this room must have been the scene of many mundane activities. Children of summer tenants must have played here. Those parallel scratches near one edge of the too-small rug probably had been made by a toy truck held in a chubby hand. Just as she had that morning, summer tenants must have taken meals over by that window, so that they could enjoy the ocean view. Most of those people probably hadn't even known that a murder had taken place here. And even if they had, it would have made no difference to many of them. She thought of how in New

York, on the day after the most horrifying murder, hundreds of apartment-hungry people would inquire about taking over the victim's lease.

That, of course, was the sensible way to look at such matters. The past was the past, shut away from the present by that most impenetrable of barriers, time.

Just the same, after this she would eat her meals in either the small dining room or the kitchen, although neither room offered an ocean view. And she would not paint here, despite that second, north-facing window. In the room directly above this one, a bedroom empty except for a double bunk bed and a chest with several drawer knobs missing, there would be even better light falling through its north window.

She turned and walked back to the kitchen. There should be about two hours of daylight left. She knew she should spend the time hanging those new curtains, but somehow she found herslef unwilling to begin the task.

She took the package of curtains up to the room she had chosen as her bedroom and left it on the bureau. Then she moved from room to room along the upstairs hallway, noticing details that had escaped her attention the evening before. A decal of Sesame Street's Big Bird, for instance, stuck to a window pane in the room with the bunk beds. An Australia-shaped leak stain on the ceiling of the bathroom with its claw-footed tub. And, at the back of the closet from which she'd taken a blanket the night before, two neat stacks of magazines on the floor. One stack consisted of copies of *The New York Review of Books*, the other of *Whispered Confessions*. She amused herself by wondering if the same person had collected both publications and if so, what sort of individual he must have been. Perhaps a

48

university professor writing a treatise on sub-species of American literature?

Directly across the hall from the closet was a room entirely empty of furniture. Doubtless it was meant to be a bedroom. Also, it was larger than the two bedrooms at the front of the house. That puzzled her, just as it had when she made her first tour of the house the evening before. Why had those two fairly small bedrooms been furnished and this one left empty? She walked to the center of the bare floor and stood looking at the faded wallpaper. Its insipid pattern of pink rosebuds against a blue background showed squares and rectangles of brighter color, where pictures must once have hung.

She became aware of how quiet it was in this back room. She couldn't hear even the ocean's murmur. She went out into the hall. As she moved along it she became aware of something else, too, an utterly unreasonable sense of another presence in the house. By the time she reached the stairs the feeling had grown so strong that she halted and swung around. There was nothing there, of course, except a beam of sunlight slanting into the hall from that empty bedroom.

This wouldn't do, she told herself. If she was going to give way to tricks of her own imagination, how could she ever hope to get completely well, emotionally as well as physically, and get on with her life?

She'd make a sketch or two, she decided. Nothing ambitious, just doodles. That always soothed her. And there would still be enough light in that room above the living room.

She descended the stairs, then reclimbed them carrying her easel and the case which held her painting and sketching material. In the room with the bunk beds she set up her easel and attached to it a square of drawing paper. Charcoal stick in hand, and wondering what to sketch, she looked out the eastern window at the ocean. The white froth of incoming wave was touched with the pale pink of near sunset.

That girl on the beach the night before, sauntering through the cold moonlight.

Kate turned to her easel. Rapidly she began to sketch the girl, not walking along the beach but standing, her face upturned to the moonlight. A few foreshortened strokes defined the slender body in its caftan, the pale, straight hair, the face with its wide-set eyes and clean-lined, somewhat squarish jaw.

A sound from downstairs. After a moment she identified it as someone knocking on the back door.

Martin Donnerly?

Even if it was, she told herself, there was nothing to worry about. Both the front and back doors were locked. She would tell him, through the door, and in the politest tone possible, that she was working and did not want to be disturbed.

And if he did not go away? Well, much as she disliked the thought, she could call that unpleasent chief of police. She laid her charcoal stick in the easel's groove, went down the stairs, and walked back along the hall to the kitchen. Through the door's glass upper half she saw that it was a woman of late middleage who stood beyond the screen.

Catching sight of Kate, the woman called, "It's only me, dear. Mrs. Thompson, Myrtle Thompson."

Myrtle Thompson. Oh, yes. The cleaning lady. Leora Kelso had said she would tell her to "drop by." Myrtle Thompson certainly had lost no time in doing so.

50

Kate unlocked the door, unhooked the screen. The woman beamed at her. "Miss Kiligrew's the name, isn't it? I had an errand over to Mockstown, and so I thought I'd stop by now. Two birds with one stone, as the fella says."

Turning her head, Kate looked past the garage at an old black sedan standing in the road. She looked back at the woman. "Come in, please."

The woman stepped into the kitchen. Thin except for wide hips, she wore brown pants of some synthetic material and a flowered top. Her face, framed by brown-gray wispy curls, was friendly but sharp-eyed. She threw a comprehensive look around the kitchen. "How often would you be wanting me, dear?"

Kate hesitated. "I really hadn't thought much about it yet. Let's see. Miss Kelso said you charge five dollars an hour."

"Yes, or I can charge by the job. When your house is clean, I leave, but not before then."

"Well, while we talk it over, wouldn't you like a cup of coffee, or some tea?"

"Thanks, dear. But I'm due in Mockstown before six. I'd have time though, to take a quick look over the house, so I could give you an idea of how much I'd have to charge you to give it a real good cleaning once a week, say." She added, "You see, I do so many houses. That's why I don't remember all the rooms here, even though I've cleaned them quite a few times."

Kate sensed that this sharp-eyed woman did remember. She was just curious about Camelot's off-season visitor. Perhaps she was one of those born-inquisitive persons, a peeker into bath cabinets and closets and, when opportunity offered, other people's letters. Perhaps she had hoped that by arriving unannounced she would find Kate

51

with luggage still only half unpacked and with articles strewn about—a bag of marijuana, for instance—that later would be put away. Such curiosity, although annoying to others, could be almost as innocent as a cat's instinct to investigate anything that came within its ken.

"All right," Kate said.

Myrtle Thompson looked into the refrigerator and into cabinet shelves and drawers, remarking now and then about how nice and clean everything was. No, she wasn't the one who'd gotten the place ready for Kate's occupancy. She'd been visiting her sister in Raleigh, and so Leora had hired someone else to get this house into shape.

Accompanied by Kate, Mrs. Thompson inspected the rest of the first floor. In the room with the fireplace, Kate saw the woman's eye go to the hook above the green-painted mantel. She made no comment, though. In all probability, Kate decided, Leora Kelso had told her cousin not to talk about that old tragedy, lest the New York girl become uneasy enough to pack her bags and leave.

They walked back to the stairwell, now filling with shadows. Kate switched on the light that illuminated the top of the stairs and the upper hall. On the second floor she led Mrs. Thompson into the room with the bunk beds. Even though daylight still lingered there, she turned on the switch that controlled the glass-shaded ceiling light.

Mrs. Thompson said, "Look at that thing pasted to the windowpane. Those are the very mischief to get off. Why some people let their kids—"

She broke off. Her gaze had shifted to the easel. She said, in a startled voice, "*You* drew that?" There was not only astonishment in her face but hostility, as if the drawing had reawakened some old animus.

52

Kate nodded.

"How on earth was it you knew Donna Sue?"

Donna Sue, the girl whose life had been ended by a shotgun blast a dozen years ago. Kate had an odd sensation, as if something cold had been drawn down her spine.

"The girl who was killed in this house? I never knew her, of course. What makes you think I did?"

Kate could tell by the confusion in the woman's face that her guess had been right. The real estate agent had warned her cousin not to talk about what had happened in this house.

"It's just that the picture you drew looks sort of like—" She leaned closer to the easel. "But I see now I was mistaken."

Kate thought the woman was going to change the subject. Instead she asked, seemingly against her will, "Who was it you were drawing?"

"A girl I saw last night." Despite the light pouring down from the ceiling, despite the woman's assertion that she had been "mistaken," Kate still felt that cold, prickling sensation, not only down her spine but over her whole body. "She was walking along the beach. She stopped and looked at this house, and the moonlight was bright enough for me to see her face quite clearly—"

Her voice trailed off. Myrtle Thompson still stared, as if fascinated, at the sketch. Then her features suddenly relaxed. "Darleen Mae," she said, and laughed.

"Darleen Mae?" The name sounded faintly familiar.

"Darleen Mae Welker, Donna Sue's twin. She wanders all over the country, any time of the day or night. As the fella says, Darleen Mae must have been standing behind the door when the brains were handed out."

In her relief, Kate had an impulse to ask, what fella was that? Instead she said, "How old is Darleen Mae?"

"Let's see. Must be thirty or a little more now. Lordy, how time flies."

"I saw her only by moonlight, of course, but she looked younger than that."

"Darleen Mae still looks like a kid. When there's not much going on in the head, not much shows on the face."

As the fella says, Kate thought. "Miss Kelso told me that the Welkers are—well, white trash was the phrase she used."

"You can say that again!" She hesitated, as if remembering Leora's instructions. But apparently her love of gossip was too much for her. She rushed on, "Worst of the lot was the oldest boy, Orren Welker. He robbed an armored truck—oh, almost fifteen years ago. He hid the money, nobody knows where, and then got himself killed in a shootout with the police. I guess the Welkers figure the money belongs to them. Anyway, I hear that every once in a while they start digging up the backwoods around that place of theirs."

She looked at her wristwatch. "Lordy! I'd better get going. Look, dear. Suppose I come here once a week. Fridays, say. I'll do whatever needs to be done, all over the house, except washing windows or waxing linoleum. For doing that, best you call my son." There was overweening pride in her voice. "He has his own cleaning service, Sonny does. He's got a truck, and a helper, and customers for miles around. But to get back to me. I'll charge you twenty-five dollars for the one-day job, even if it takes me as much as eight hours."

Compared to the going rate for such services in New York, twenty-five dollars was almost embarrassingly low. "That will be fine, Mrs. Thompson."

"I'll need some things. I notice somebody must have taken the scrub brush and the dust mop. And I'll need more soap flakes and scrubbing powder than you've got under the sink now."

"I'll see to all that."

She accompanied the woman downstairs and bade her good night.

Returning to the upstairs room, she looked with pity at the unfinished sketch on the easel. Darleen Mae Welker, Donna Sue's brain-damaged twin. What sort of vague notions must have been floating through that exquisite head as she wandered through the night?

Kate detached the sketch from the easel, ripped it into four pieces, and looked around the room for a wastebasket. There was none. Well, she'd buy some within the next few days. She carried the ripped sketch downstairs, put it in the trash basket under the sink, and then broiled a lamb chop and cooked some frozen string beans for her dinner.

CHAPTER EIGHT

The next few days were quite pleasant, with mostly sunny skies and temperatures more like those Kate had expected to find in North Carolina in March. She hung curtains, went into the little town for wastebaskets and for Mrs. Thompson's cleaning materials, and made leisurely tours along the dirt road that encircled the island. She found that the island seemed to be tipped slightly toward the east, with low cliffs on its western shore and flat, mostly rocky beaches on the side that received the Atlantic's waves, low rollers whose forward rush had been slowed by a hidden off-shore sandbar.

As she drove, she made mental notes of spots where she might set up her easel, once she had persuaded herself to start painting. She had never attempted landscapes in oil. Perhaps her reluctance to go to work was due to a fear of discovering that, after all, her talents were restricted to commercial art.

Martin Donnerly did not come near the house again, at least as far as she knew. Once she caught a glimpse of him leaving the bank in Camelot. He did not see her. Again she recalled the tension in Vanessa Weyant's voice and long-fingered hands as, holding the forms Kate had just made out, she talked of Martin Donnerly. Could it be that the woman, under that cool, chic surface, had been in love with a convicted murderer, and perhaps still was?

Somehow Kate did not find the idea at all preposterous.

On Wednesday afternoon, in the grocery store in Camelot, she placed her purchases on the checkout counter and then noticed a stack of newspapers beside the cash register. Large type across the top of the front page announced that it was the *Camelot Weekly Clarion*. She added a copy to her other purchases.

That night, while eating her dinner of salad and broiled fish—local fish, and wonderfully fresh—she read the *Clarion*. She felt surprise that such a small community should have such an excellent newspaper. It was well-written, and Kate did not spot a single typographical error. There were of course many items of purely local interest, such as news of Ronnie Dack's tenth birthday party and Mr. and Mrs. Gerald Smiths' trip to Wilmington to see Mrs. Smith's sister. But there was also a well-organized and even lively account of the State Legislature's hearing on coastal erosion. The editorial column was concerned not only with whether or not the town should install parking meters before the start of the summer season, but also with the need for more supplements to national health insurance.

Kate looked at the masthead. The *Camelot Weekly Clarion*, formerly the *Blackfish Island Clarion*, had been founded more than fifty years ago. Its present publisher and editor, surely not the same man as its founder, was Chadwick Garner.

She wondered about him. Why should a man of such obvious ability and wide-ranging interests choose to publish a newspaper in a small, almost moribund community like Camelot?

On Friday morning Myrtle Thompson arrived at eight o'clock. She proved to be not only a rapid and thorough housecleaner but also a highly vocal one, with a large repertoire of Protestant hymns. While she attacked the sink with scouring powder she sang loudly and offkey, "What a Friend We Have in Jesus." While she wielded a dust mop in the dining room she sang, not inappropriately, "Brighten the Corner Where You Are." Kate decided that late-teenage domestic workers she had encountered in New York, who toiled with transistors set at top volume, hadn't been so bad after all. Finally, after a lunch during which Myrtle talked nonstop about her boy Sonny and his house cleaning business, Kate put her painting gear in the VW and fled.

She drove to a spot on the western side of the island where a path curved down the face of a low cliff. A blue pickup truck stood a few feet beyond the entrance to the path. There must be a fisherman down there on the beach. No matter. In fact, perhaps she would put him in her painting. And the air seemed still on this side of the island, which meant it would be a good day to paint outdoors. Easel and folded tripod under one arm and paint-and-brush case carried in the other hand, she descended the gentle slope to the beach.

A moment before she reached it a man seated on a driftwood log near the cliff's base got to his feet. In his hand was a sandwich, still wrapped in plastic. A paperback book lay face down on the log.

59

Kate and Martin Donnerly looked at each other through the early afternoon sunlight. His expression, somber and sardonic, told her that he realized that by this time she must have heard where he had spent the last twelve years.

She said, "Hello."

He nodded. "Are you going to paint?"

"I'm going to try."

"Well, don't let me disturb you. I was about to leave anyway." He bent, picked up his book.

"You were not!" Until she heard her own voice, she hadn't known she was going to say that. She added, in a more matter-of-fact tone, "It's obvious you came down here to read your book while you ate lunch. There's no reason why you shouldn't do just that."

"I can just as well eat in my truck."

"Please!" She felt obscurely angry. "If you leave, you *will* be disturbing me. Upsetting me, I mean. So please."

His voice and his dark blue eyes were expressionless now. "Very well." He sat down on the log.

She moved closer to the water, thinking that he might get to his feet and hurry after her to help her set up the easel. He did not. She drove the tripod's legs an inch or so into the sand and then placed on the easel a blank canvas she had prepared a few days earlier.

She looked out over the blue water. Even on this windless day its movements, so slight as to be almost imperceptible, made it sparkle like some million-faceted gem. Between the island and the mainland, its pine-covered shore looking almost black, two small boats, probably fishing vessels, moved slowly.

She set to work. She would try something minimalist, she decided. A strip of yellow in the foreground to indicate the beach. Then a broad stretch of blue, with just a suggestion of gray-hulled boats and their square super-structures. Beyond that a strip of black shoreline.

It wouldn't work. The painting refused to come to life. Was it because of Martin Donnerly? He must still be back there. She hadn't heard the truck drive away. After a while she stole a look over her shoulder. Yes, he was still there, head bent over his book. But she had the feeling that a split second before he had been watching her.

She painted for a few minutes more, then gave up. Illustrations she had made for gingerale or bath powder ads had had more life in them than this. Exasperated, she took the canvas from the easel and laid it face up on the sand. Kneeling, she repacked her paints and brushes.

His footsteps over the sand had been noiseless. She wasn't aware of his presence beside her until he said, "Leaving?"

With a start, she looked up to see him looming over her. For a moment she felt a terrified awareness, not just in her mind but in her shrinking nerves, that this man looking down at her had served a long prison sentence for killing a woman. Then the moment of fear passed. According to what people said, he'd had reasons for feeling a murderous rage toward his wife. He had no reason for wanting to harm her.

But that flash of fear must have shown in her face, because his own face took on a remote look. "Sorry I startled you. It occurred to me that you might want some help carrying that stuff up the cliff."

61

"Oh! Thank you." She got to her feet, brushed sand from the knees of her jeans, and then picked up the unfinished painting. "I'd better carry this. Not that it would be any loss if it got smeared."

"Something wrong with it?"

"It's no good, that's all." She held it out to him. "See for yourself."

Holding the canvas in his hands—deeply browned hands, like his neck and face—he looked down at it. "I'm afraid I don't know much about this sort of thing."

She wasn't deceived. She could tell he didn't think much of it either. He added, handing the canvas back to her, "Maybe you weren't in the right mood."

"And maybe I don't have what it takes to be more than what I am." To save him the need to reply to that, she went on, "Not that I mind too much. I enjoy my work, and so I'm grateful for what talent I do have."

He folded the tripod and tucked it under his arm, then lifted the paint-and-brush case. She said, "This is kind of you. Once you've lugged all this up the path, you can read your book in peace."

Neither of them had made any move to start toward the cliff. He said, "No, I was intending to walk down the beach about a quarter of a mile. I'm going to build my boatyard there."

She said, "Why are you—" and then stopped, dismayed by her own lack of tact.

"Why am I what?"

She said, floundering, "It's just that I would have thought—I mean, didn't you think of going someplace else to—"

62

"To start all over again? No, I prefer to finish what I started here. I intended to build a boatyard on this island and by God that's what I'm going to do."

"But—but why is it so important to you to—"

"Because I'm determined to get back all that I can! I can't get the twelve years back. But I can carry out the plans I'd made before I—"

He broke off for a moment, and then went on, "If I were guilty, I suppose I would want to go somewhere for a new start. But as it is, I'm going to stay right here. I'll never be able to convince people on this island that I didn't kill my wife. But at least I can stand my ground instead of running."

A dizzying relief swept through her. Then she had the dismayed realization that he could be lying now, just as a jury had thought twelve years ago that he was lying then. And anyway, why should it mean so much to her to have him say that he was innocent?

Nevertheless, she found herself asking, "Then you didn't—"

"No. I don't suppose I would ever be able to convince you of it, but I didn't."

Through a silence broken only by the cries of two seagulls wheeling overhead, she looked into his somber face. Then she said, "You could try."

"Try?"

"To convince me. You could tell me about it."

His lips thinned. For a moment she thought he was going to say, "Why should I?"

Instead he said, "You mean right now?"

"If you want to."

After a moment he said, "I suppose I'll be just making a damn fool of myself, but I guess I do want to. Where shall we talk? Back there on that log?"

Kate nodded.

CHAPTER
NINE

In silence they walked across the upward-sloping beach, she holding the unfinished canvas, he with the tripod and easel and carrying case. When they reached the foot of the cliff she looked down at the outspread paperback, lying face down on the silvery log. It was *Moby Dick*.

She said, sitting down on the log, "Somehow I could never get very far in that book."

He deposited her painting gear carefully on the sand and then sat down beside her. "A lot of people can't. But you really should read the chapter 'The Whiteness of the Whale.' It's a knockout."

"Maybe I will try to read it sometime."

For a few moments they looked out over the water. The fishing boats were still there, gray against the dark mainland. Then he said, "It's obvious that you've already heard something about my wife's death."

Did he know that she had consulted that dreadful police chief about him? She hoped not. "Well, I have heard a little. For instance, I know that your wife's name was Donna Sue."

"Yes, Donna Sue Welker." He picked up a handful of sand and funneled it out of a loosely curled fist. "She was beautiful."

Kate said nothing.

"I fell in love with her the first time I saw her. There was a diner in Camelot then. She'd just gone to work there, driving over the causeway every day from the Welker place on the other side of Mockstown. I'd come home for the summer after my freshman year in college. We were the same age, eighteen."

He paused, looking out over the water. Kate wondered what he was really seeing. Donna Sue handing him a sandwich across the diner's counter? Donna Sue's face as he held her in his arms in some parked car, or on a moonflooded beach, or deep in the pine woods on the mainland?

"Until then I'd expected to go to Baltimore or Philadelphia after I got my degree in marine engineering. I thought I'd build my career slowly, starting on the bottom rung of some big ship building company. But after I met Donna Sue, that idea went out the window. I wanted to marry her just as soon as I could. I felt that was the only way I could hope to hold onto her. God, you should have seen how men looked at her. Not just the young guys. Vacationers who came here, married men in the town, everyone.

"I'd have married her right then if she'd said yes, and worked at any sort of job to support us. But she said she'd never marry some garage mechanic or grocery clerk, so in the fall I went back to college. The next three years were hell. Donna Sue would mention other men in her letters. Once she wrote that some Hollywood agent had shown up at the diner. He'd left his powerboat in some marina down

66

the coast after its engine had conked out. While it was being repaired, he'd been driving around the countryside in a rented car. When he saw Donna Sue he offered to pay her way to the Coast and arrange a screen test for her. When she wrote me that, I left college in the middle of the week and drove hell-for-leather back here."

He broke off. After a moment Kate asked, "And the Hollywood agent?"

"He'd left. Donna Sue said she'd found out he was a phony, an office supplies' salesman from Atlanta. I'm not sure but what she made up the whole thing just to bring me hotfooting back here. She got a kick out of doing things like that."

Again he stopped speaking. Kate asked, "When did you marry her?"

"As soon as I finished college. My father and my brother David—he's a year younger than me—were dead set against it. It wasn't just because of her reputation. It was—"

Kate waited a moment and then asked, "It was what?"

For the first time he sounded embarrassed. "Her people. The Welkers are backwoods types. And the Donnerlys—well, a hundred-and-sixty years ago they were poor farmers back in Ireland. But they came to this country well before the Civil War, managed to buy some land cheap, and started growing tobacco. They were both hardworking and lucky, I guess. Anyway, they not only made money but managed to hold onto it even after the War. In the nineteen-twenties my grandfather sold off most of the land and put the money in the stock market. He too was lucky. He got out just before the Crash. My father didn't make a lot of money—he had a law practice in

67

Mockstown—but there was still the money inherited from my grandfather. Besides, by that time the Donnerlys had established themselves as—well—"

"Quality?"

For the first time that day she saw a smile touch his lips. "I guess you could call it that." The smile vanished. "I wanted my father to loan me enough to build a boatyard, but he turned me down flat. So I took a job in the Camelot garage, sure that in a year or so I'd be able to save the money I needed."

"I don't understand. Couldn't you and Donna Sue have gone to Baltimore or someplace where you could have gotten a better job? After all, you had a degree."

"She didn't want to leave this area. She was too attached to her family, although God knows why. But then, lots of people around here tend to be clannish." He stopped for a moment and then went on, "So we got married and moved into the Hillier house. It was more rent than I wanted to pay. After all, there was a small apartment above the variety store. That would have been big enough for us. But she liked the idea of a large house, maybe because she'd grown up with seven people living in a three-room shack."

He fell silent, looking out over the water. A breeze had come up, strong enough to kick up a few whitecaps and set the masts of the fishing boats to swaying.

"From the first," he said, "we fought a lot. Sometimes it was over money. She was extravagant. She was always sending away for mail order clothes, most of it pretty shoddy stuff, or buying god-awful lamps and ornaments from the variety store. She wanted me to get ahead, but she couldn't seem to understand that I was going to need capital, and that the only way to get it was to save it.

"Most of our quarrels, though," he went on, "were over men. I'd thought that when she'd quit her job, something she was only too glad to do, I wouldn't have to worry about other guys. But she wasn't content to stay home. I guess I was crazy to think she would be. After all, we were both only twenty-one. She bought an old car in Mockstown—the dealer practically gave it to her—and after that she spent her days with the Welkers or roaming over the countryside. She insisted that all she did was to drive around, but I kept hearing rumors—"

He broke off. The silence lengthened until it became almost painfully awkward. A seagull landed nearby and walked back and forth, eyeing them. Then, apparently convinced that they were not going to throw him any food, he flew off.

"The night that it—happened," Martin said, "started off just fine. It was a Friday night in July. My boss at the garage had planned to send me on an overnight trip to Norfolk to look at a used hydraulic lift, but at the last minute he changed his mind. After work I bought a bottle of wine—Donna Sue loved little surprises like that—and took it home. I figured we wouldn't have dinner in the kitchen that night. She'd set the table in the dining room, the way she sometimes did on weekends. We'd drink our wine with dinner. And after a while we'd make love. Maybe we'd spread a blanket on the little bit of lawn in front of the house. We did that sometimes on hot summer nights.

"We had lamb stew for dinner. Donna Sue wasn't much of a housekeeper, but she was a good cook. We drank our wine. Then she said she'd bring in our dessert from the refrigerator.

"The stew had been spicy, and so in spite of the wine I

was thirsty. I went into the kitchen to get a drink of water. She wasn't there. Then I heard the sound of the phone being dialed. I went out into the hall. There she was in that alcove under the stairs, holding the handset to her ear. At sight of me she put the phone down in its cradle. She was just checking the time, she said. Donna Sue could tell a lie well if she'd had time to prepare it. She wasn't much good at spur-of-the-moment lying.

"I demanded to know who she'd been trying to call. When she persisted in that silly story about checking the time, I said she must have made a date with someone, thinking I'd be away overnight. Now she'd been trying to call the guy to warn him off.

"We began to yell at each other. Finally she ran up the stairs to our room, with me right behind her. In the bedroom she picked up her handbag from the dresser. I took it away from her, took her car keys out of it, and put them in my pocket. She flew at me, and raked her fingernails down my face. I shoved her away so hard that she staggered and fell, striking her cheek against the dresser's edge. I ran out of the house and got into my car. I drove across the causeway and just kept driving in various directions until almost midnight. Finally I drove home and went into the house by the back door."

Again there was silence. Then he began to speak very rapidly. He'd found the kitchen all torn up, he said, with canned goods swept from the shelves and tumbled onto the sinkboard, coffee and sugar containers emptied into the sink, refrigerator door left open. And in the living room he'd found Donna Sue, lying on the floor on her back.

"The shotgun was beside her. It was one I'd owned since I was thirteen. Usually it hung by a strap from a hook above the fireplace mantel. Someone—someone had emptied both barrels into her chest and face."

He must have told that story over and over again, Kate thought, to the police, and on the witness stand, and perhaps now and then to a fellow convict. And yet his voice still held a sickened horror.

He had telephoned the police station, he told her. "Chief Bosley and the deputy then came. They looked over the rest of the house and found that it too had been torn up. Dresser drawers had been emptied out and clothes from Donna Sue's closet thrown on the floor with the pockets turned inside out. They asked me a lot of questions. Then they arrested me."

"Didn't they even warn you about your rights to keep silent, and to have an attorney, and all that?"

"Oh, yes." Again he gave that faint smile. "Not even Chief Bosley is that far behind the times. But I *wanted* to talk. You see, in my first shock, it seemed to me impossible that anyone could believe I had killed Donna Sue."

"But they did."

"They did. And weeks and weeks later, after listening to all the evidence against me, I wasn't surprised by the jury's verdict. If someone I knew had seen me during those hours I'd been driving aimlessly around, it might have helped. But no one had seen me. The fingerprints on the gun were either mine or too blurred to be classified. It was obvious that Donna Sue and I had had a fight. Skin from my face was under her fingernails, and despite those shotgun pellets the county medical examiner had been able to tell that her cheek had been badly bruised sometime before her death. The prosecutor argued that I had shot her in a jealous rage, then gone over the house

71

emptying out drawers and ripping sofa cushions and mattresses and so on, so that it would look as if a burglar or some other intruder had done it. And after I'd done all that, he said, I called the police."

Silence settled down. A few yards offshore a gull, perhaps the same one who had been eyeing them, dove into the wind-ruffled water and came up with a small fish wriggling in its beak.

Kate said, "Who do you think killed her?"

"I don't know." Suddenly he sounded very tired. "She'd given a lot of guys besides me a rough time. And of course there were wives and girl friends who had reason to hate her. And too, there was the money that one of her brother's stole."

Myrtle Thompson had said something about Donna Sue's brother. "You mean the one who robbed a bank?"

"Not a bank. An armored car. He hid the money someplace and then got himself killed in a shootout with the police. That happened three years before Donna Sue and I were married. The police never located the money. When Chief Bosley came back downstairs that night Donna Sue—died and told me the second floor was torn up too, it flashed through my mind that maybe someone had been looking for the armored car money. Maybe the Welkers, or at least one of them, had the money all along, and had thought maybe it would be safer hidden in our house than on the Welker place. Then maybe someone else who knew it was in our house came to take it—"

His voice trailed off. Then he said, "My lawyer suggested that idea to the jury, but it didn't fly. By then they were thoroughly convinced that I'd torn up the house myself, to try to throw the police off the track."

He stopped speaking. Up on the road a car passed, and Kate wondered if its driver had noticed her VW and Martin's pickup parked close to each other. After a moment he turned his face toward her. "Well?"

"I believe you." She hoped it wasn't just because she wanted to believe him.

Some of the tension went out of his dark face, but all he said was, "You want me to carry this stuff up to your car?"

At the top of the low cliff, after he'd stowed her painting gear in the little car's trunk, she turned to him, one hand holding the unsatisfactory canvas. "I've seen you only once in Camelot. Are you staying there?"

"No, I'm staying at my brother's house. But now that I've got the bank loan for my boatyard, I'll be over here a lot."

His brother's house, not his father's. "Is your father—"

"He died while I was inside."

And, apparently, he had willed the ancestral home to his younger son. Had David Donnerly inherited the other family assets too? He must have. Otherwise Martin would not have had to apply for a bank loan.

She wondered what the imprisoned Martin must have felt like when he first learned that he had lost even his birthright.

She said impulsively, "My phone's connected. If you'd like me to fix lunch for us someday, just call me."

The look that leaped into his eyes told her how much he valued the invitation. Then the look faded. "Thank you very much, but I'm going to be quite busy from now on."

She said, somewhat stiffly, "Yes, I suppose you will be."

He held the paperback book out to her. "Take this. As I said, even if you read only the whiteness of the whale chapter—"

Then he did intend to see her again. "Thank you. I'll take good care of it."

"You don't have to. I don't want it back. There's a hardcover copy at the house, my brother's house, I mean. I just bought the paperback to read on the bus the day I—started back here."

He meant from prison. She said, "You're so very tanned."

"You mean for someone who's been in stir. I had a good job my last two years there. Assistant to the groundskeeper. Well, goodbye."

"Goodbye. Thanks again for carrying my things."

CHAPTER
TEN

Despite Martin's assertion that he would be "busy," she kept expecting during the next few days that he would telephone. He did not.

She cooked and ate her solitary meals, and walked up and down the rocky beach that stretched in front of the house. She read a P.D. James thriller from the circulating library in Camelot's only drugstore, and she read Melville's chapter, "The Whiteness of the Whale." The beauty of its imagery fascinated her. Its philosophy appalled her. How terrible to feel, as Melville apparently did, that the universe at heart was either bleakly uncaring, like a vast Arctic waste, or actually malevolent toward man, like the great white whale Captain Ahab pursued.

If Martin had adopted that philosophy, when had he done so? Surely not as a very young man. She thought of the twenty-one-year-old Martin Donnerly beating out all rivals to marry his Donna Sue, working long hours, and trying to save money to build his boatyard. Obviously that Martin had felt both enthusiastic and confident. It must have been the imprisoned Martin who had accepted Melville's bleak view of reality.

She spent two afternoons on the beach where she and Martin had talked. As she took another stab at painting the view toward the mainland, she kept thinking that he might drive past, see her VW parked on the cliff, and stop. He did not appear.

Twice she saw him in Camelot. Once again he was coming out of the bank. As nearly as she could tell, he did not see her. Another time he drove past in his pickup truck while she was getting into her parked car. He smiled slightly and waved, but did not stop.

One morning as she sat on the doorstep, drinking her breakfast coffee in the breeze-cooled sunlight, something near the base of the house's old cement foundation caught her eye. Between two daffodil shoots, now in bud, was a little reddish-brown heap of what looked like rusted metal. Setting down her coffee cup, she went over to investigate.

When she had picked it up she saw that it had once been a charm bracelet. Rust had fused its links together and so deeply encrusted the charms that it was only with difficulty that she identified one as a heart, another as a tiny automobile, another as a guitar or perhaps a banjo.

It must have been lying there for years. She recalled what Martin had said about his wife's habit of buying "god-awful" ornaments at the variety store. This bracelet of some corrodible metal might have come from there. Chances were, though, that it had not belonged to Donna Sue. Many other people over the years had occupied this house for varying lengths of time.

She let the bracelet fall back among the daffodil shoots.

Later that day she went into town for groceries. When

her shopping was finished she went into the Bluebell Café for a cup of coffee. As she sat at the counter, Vanessa Weyant slipped onto the stool beside her. "Hello, there. How are you making out?"

Kate smiled at her. She thought of how much more at home Vanessa would look at the Four Seasons than in this lunchroom.

"Has Martin Donnerly shown up at your place again?"

The tone was light, the manner poised. And yet as Kate looked at the woman with the sleek cap of dark hair and the beautifully tended skin and the determined-looking jaw, she thought, why, she *is* in love with Martin! Probably she has been for years.

What must Vanessa have felt when Martin's lovely and promiscuous young wife died in that dreadful fashion? Shock, of course. But had she also felt a secret gladness, a secret hope?

Kate said, "No, he hasn't been there."

The middle-aged waitress brought Vanessa's diet cola. For perhaps five minutes they chatted about various topics, the skirt, an English import, which Vanessa was wearing, and a dramatic series, also English, which had appeared on Public Television the previous fall. Then Kate paid for her coffee, said goodbye, and left.

Vanessa watched her go. She knew that Martin and the New York girl had spent some time together on the beach one day recently. Driving along that road, she had seen the VW and Martin's pickup parked at the top of the cliff. She'd driven a few yards, stopped, and walked back along the cliff's edge. How humiliated she had felt to be spying! But she'd been unable to resist the impulse.

They had been sitting down there on a drift log. Even though they sat well apart, Vanessa could tell that the New York girl was listening intently to whatever he was saying.

A few minutes ago she had given Kate an opportunity to say, "No, he hasn't come to the house, but we talked on the beach a few days ago." The girl had chosen to remain silent about that meeting, which must mean that it had held more than casual significance for her.

Vanessa's hand tightened around her cola glass. She'd have to do something about that. After all the lonely, waiting years, she wasn't going to let some chit of a stranger snare Martin's interest. She drained her glass, laid coins on the counter, and went back to the bank.

CHAPTER ELEVEN

That night Kate dreamed that she and Martin were driving along a strange road in a car that was neither his pickup truck nor her VW. He stopped the car and took her in his arms. From that point on, the dream was so frankly erotic that she awoke in the dawn light, feeling dismayed.

This wouldn't do. In the first place, even though he might feel attracted to her, Martin obviously meant to stay away from her. In the second and far more important place, she could not be sure that Martin hadn't killed his faithless wife. She hoped he had not, and, as she had told him, she believed he had not. But there was no way under the sun for her to be absolutely sure.

She might be able to decide more firmly, though, one way or the other, if she could learn more about what had happened twelve years ago. Not just from Martin himself, and not from Vanessa Weyant, who perhaps for her own reasons might want Kate to shun him as a killer. If there were just some disinterested source—

She thought of that surprisingly excellent little newspaper, the *Camelot Weekly Clarion.* It had been in existence twelve years ago, very likely under its present editorship. If he would let her read his file of back copies—

Shortly before noon she parked the VW in a vacant place in front of the drugstore and then walked a few yards to the *Clarion* office. It was in a red brick building with what was apparently an apartment—she could see white curtains at the windows—on the second floor. As she passed the newspaper's plate glass window she saw a sandy-haired man inside. He sat reading a newspaper. His feet, crossed at the ankles, rested on his desk.

She turned into the little entryway. Ahead of her stairs led upward. To her left was a door with the black-painted words, "*Camelot Weekly Clarion*. Please enter."

She opened the door and walked in. Smiling, the sandy-haired man got to his feet with the newspaper still in his hand. He appeared to be in his mid-forties, an attractive man of medium height with gray eyes set in a thin, sensitive-looking face.

"Mr. Chadwick Garner?"

"That's right, although most people shorten it to Chad. And you're Miss Kiligrew." His smile broadened. "Don't look so surprised. I'm sure everyone in town knew who you were before you'd been here twenty-four hours." He laid the paper—*The New York Times,* she noticed—on his desk and then indicated the straight chair opposite his swivel one.

From beyond the doorway to what was probably the pressroom, a rhythmic slamming noise began. He said, raising his voice slightly, "Won't you sit down?"

When they were both seated he said, "I hope you've brought me some news. I'm running low on items this week. Only one birthday and one engagement. One arrest—Chief Bosley took one of our two town drunks into custody again. Belle and Charlie Crowe have their daughter and son-in-law from Nashville visiting them, and the Todd Marshalls are going to spend Easter with Mrs. Marshall's brother in Philadelphia. If people don't start walking in with more news I'm going to have to get out the back files and compose one of those twenty-years-ago-this-week-in-Camelot columns."

She smiled. "Is that why you're sitting out here right in your front window?"

"Like a spider in its web? Yes, that's why. People drop in just to chat, but pretty soon they say something I can turn into a few sticks of type."

"Well, I'm sorry to disappoint you, but I've come here to get information, not give it." She hesitated. "I've been wondering if I could look up a court case in your back issues, a—a murder case."

He said, after a moment, "You must mean the Donnerly case. It's the one murder this town ever had. But good lord, that was a dozen years ago."

"I know."

"Do you mind my asking why you're interested?"

She felt color in her face. "Just idle curiosity, I guess. I mean, I rented the house where it happened."

No, he thought. It wasn't just idle curiosity. A girl that empty-headed wouldn't have thought of consulting a newspaper's back files. Besides, there was that color dyeing those nice high cheekbones of hers.

It must be Donnerly then. A girl like this, attractive and intelligent, interested in a man who'd spent twelve years in prison.

Was it Graham Greene who said that God must have

81

been in a sardonically humorous mood when he invented sex? Whoever said it, he reflected wryly, had hit the nail right on the head.

"Of course you can look at the files. Better use the back office, though. Otherwise the citizenry will be coming in just to find out what you're doing here."

She accompanied him into the next room, where a blond youth with acne scars on his cheeks and an ink smudge on his chin fed green rectangles of paper, evidently for some kind of poster, into an ancient flatbed press. "Job printing," Chad Garner said. "Scarcely a part of the romance of journalism, but it does help to pay the bills."

In the room beyond the pressroom only a little gray light filtered through what was evidently an alley window. He switched on a green-shaded drop light that dangled above a long table. The table was bare except for two file cases of dark green metal. "Have a seat."

She sat down in the only chair drawn up to the table. He went through a doorless entrance to a still smaller room. When he switched on the light there she saw wall shelves filled with tall volumes bound in dark blue cloth.

After a couple of minutes he brought in a volume and, after blowing dust from its top edge, laid it on the table and leafed rapidly through it. A banner headline, "Local Girl Slain; Husband Held," seemed to leap up into her face.

"There it is, the July fifteenth issue. You'll find everything in this volume. It runs through the following March, and by then Donnerly had been tried and sentenced. Well, I'm going back to do my spider act. I'll drop back soon, though, to see how you're getting along."

He walked away. Kate bent over the outspread volume. Swiftly she read how Melvin Bosley had received a telephone call from Martin Donnerly soon after midnight, and how he had picked up his deputy and driven to the Donnerly residence. There he had found Donna Sue Donnerly dead on the floor, with a shotgun beside her, and her young husband with long scratches on his face, and much of the house turned upside down. The story in that issue ended with Martin's arrest.

The case took up even more space the next week. There was a picture of Donna Sue's coffin being carried out of a Mockstown church. The caption identified two of the pallbearers as her brothers, Elvin and Earl Welker. By that time reporters from Raleigh and Wilmington had arrived, apparently assigned to the case because the dead girl had been beautiful, and because the accused's family had long been prominent in the region. Chad Garner had interviewed the big-city reporters and had managed to fill several columns with their comments on Camelot and small-town newspapers. As for Martin, he had by then been transferred to the jail in Mockstown, the county seat.

For the next several issues the stories were briefer. Kate read of Martin's indictment and of how his father, Martin Donnerly, Senior, "member of one of the county's leading families and a prominent attorney," had hired a famous criminal lawyer to defend his son.

In mid-September the trial had begun. A number of witnesses, among them Vanessa Weyant and Martin's employer at the garage, had testified that he was of sound character. Martin's lawyer managed to get it into the record that Donna Sue, on the other hand, had had a reputation for promiscuity. The defense contended that any one of many men, including the person Donna Sue had tried to telephone that night, could have killed her. Furthermore, the defense lawyer pointed out, her death could have been connected in some way with the armored car robbery perpetrated by the eldest Welker son, Orren, three years earlier.

All the famous lawyer's expensive skill did no good. After all, there was no evidence, beyond Martin's own statement, that Donna Sue had tried to make a phone call that night. There was no evdence that any of her oldest brother's criminal loot had ever been in her possession. All the evidence there was—the scratches on Martin's face, the absence of any identifiable prints but his own on the shotgun, and the absence of any fingerprints but his and Donna Sue's anywhere in the house—all pointed to a physical struggle which had ended in her death.

Still, the jury must have felt some sympathy for Martin. Otherwise the verdict would have been first-degree murder, not second.

Kate closed the volume and then just sat there in the glare of the droplight, staring at two framed photographs on the far wall. She felt a dull disappointment. Probably it had been unreasonable of her, but she had hoped that a contemporary account would enable her to come to some final judgment about his guilt or innocence. It had not. Just as before, she wanted to believe Martin's version of events but could not, at least not beyond that nagging little doubt.

She got up from the table and walked across the room for a closer look at those framed photographs. One of them showed Chad Garner, younger but still recognizable, standing beside a gray-haired, smiling man with an unmistakable look of power. Across the bottom of the photograph someone had written in black ink, "Governor Simon Weems with State Legislator Chadwick Garner."

The second showed Chad and a pretty young woman standing on what looked like the Capitol steps in Washington. With them was a robust-looking man whom Kate vaguely recognized even before she read the handwritten caption: "The Vice-President and Chad and Louise Garner."

She heard footsteps. The *Clarion's* editor and publisher came in. "Finished?"

"Yes, thank you."

"Find anything you didn't know before?"

"Not much." She hesitated and then asked, "Do you think he was guilty?"

He frowned. "I know what you mean. There's always a doubt when the evidence is purely circumstantial. But then, it usually is, isn't it? Not many people commit murder in front of witnesses."

"I suppose not." Then, wanting to change the subject: "So you're a politico as well as a newspaper man?"

"Was, some years ago. Politics and small-town journalism mix well. Two years after I bought the *Clarion*, I ran for the state legislature and won. That was fifteen years ago. I was the next to the youngest member of the legislature."

"You didn't run again?"

"Oh, yes. And I won. But the third time I got licked."

"What happened?"

"My opponent campaigned almost entirely on one issue, prayer in the schools."

"He was for it?"

"Yes. I advanced the usual opposing argument—you know, that school prayer violates the separation of church and state. The church and the home were the places for organized prayer, I said. School was the place for learning spelling and algebra. I held my own with that argument until I got carried away in a public debate. If school prayer would be such a nostrum for all our social ills, why confine organized prayer to the schools? Why not prayer in supermarkets and football stadiums? Why not do as the Moslems do, and have ministers standing atop tall towers to lead the entire populace in prayer a couple of times a day? My opponent shouted that I was ridiculing the Christian religion and so must be some kind of atheist. That tipped the balance against me."

"Too bad."

He shrugged. "I got over it."

"Did your wife mind?"

"Not much. She was already sick then." He paused. "She died a year later. Breast cancer."

"Oh, I'm sorry."

He nodded an acknowledgment, walked over to the table, and closed the volume of back issues. Kate hesitated and then asked, "Did you know Martin Donnerly's wife?"

"Donna Sue? Of course."

"What was she like?"

"Amoral. Not immoral. Just without any morals at all. I don't think it ever occurred to her that it might be wrong to go after something or someone she wanted. Her wanting it was all the justification she needed."

"But she was lovely to look at?"

"Gorgeous. I doubt that there was a man for miles around, no matter how much he loved another woman, who didn't throw a lecherous thought in Donna Sue's direction now and then."

Kate smiled. "Did that include you?"

"Sure." He carried the tall volume into the little sideroom and restored it to its shelf.

Kate said, "I'll be going now. Thank you very much."

They walked together through the press room, which was empty now, and into the front office. At the door they shook hands. Chad Garner stood at the window to watch her walk to her car. Nice girl. Pretty too. Great legs. He had an impulse to hurry after her and ask her to lunch.

Instead he walked back to his desk, sat down, and picked up the *Times*. After the bad years, his life was back on track again. In a few months he would announce his candidacy, not for the State Legislature this time, but for the U.S. Congress. Over the years he'd given enough lectures at journalism schools around the state, shaken enough hands, endorsed enough candidates, that he could be sure of fairly broad support.

And he was engaged to a girl in Raleigh, the niece of that silver-haired governor whose photograph hung on the wall in the rear office. Stephanie was not only well-connected, but attractive. He loved her. Oh, not the way he had loved his first wife. But enough that their marriage ought to be a success.

He was still young, as ages are considered in politics, and comparatively healthy. True, he'd had a heart attack five years ago, but he had recovered nicely. Oh, a little breathlessness when he climbed to his apartment above the newspaper office, but nothing more. With Stephanie beside him, no telling how far he might go, maybe all the way to the top. This was no time to give in to that wayward libido of his.

Opening the paper to the editorial page, he laughed

87

at himself inwardly. Politics was like cocaine. Once you'd held office, you were hooked. Why, probably there wasn't an election winner in this country, even if all he'd won was a town clerkship, who didn't now and then entertain a secret dream of himself striding to a podium while the Marine Band played "Hail to the Chief."

CHAPTER TWELVE

During the next few days Kate came to regret having read those back issues of the *Clarion*. They had brought her no additional reason for believing in Martin Donnerly's version of what had happened that long ago summer night. All they had done was make the events of that night seem even more disturbingly vivid to her.

She began to feel a return of the sensation she had experienced her second day here, a sense of another presence in the house. It would steal over her as she moved about the kitchen preparing her dinner, or when she sat beneath the dining room droplight with its fake Tiffany shade, or when she climbed the stairs toward her bedroom. Because she realized that it must be just a trick of her nerves, she would concentrate her attention on something else, anything else—her own reflection in the window above the kitchen sink, or the look of her hands wielding a knife and fork, or a threadbare spot on the brown stair runner. After a moment the sensation would fade, then vanish.

But she found no way to keep herself from dreaming of Martin. Most of the dreams were not too disturbing.

Once they strolled along the beach below that cliff, talking of matters she could not recall when she woke up. Another time, for reasons known only to her unconscious mind, she and Martin were aboard a Staten Island ferry. But twice more she had dreams of them making love, dreams so vividly frank that, upon awakening, she felt aghast.

Another dream was highly disturbing in a different way. One night, torn from deep sleep, she sat bolt upright in bed. *Had* there been a scream downstairs, followed by an explosive noise?

She listened. The house was so quiet that she could hear the rapid thud of her own heart, mingling with the tick of the little travel clock on the nightstand. A dream, she told herslef. Go back to sleep.

But of course she found that she could not go back to sleep. Finally she descended the stairs, switched on the overhead light in the living room. Its glare revealed the room to be empty and in perfect order.

On Friday morning Myrtle Thompson arrived while Kate was still eating her breakfast of toast and jam and coffee in the kitchen. The woman looked around her at the gleaming refrigerator, the spotless sink, the dish towels hanging evenly on their rack. "You've sure kept this place clean." She sounded a bit disgruntled. "I don't see how you could have got much painting done."

"I haven't felt like painting." The truth was that she had tried, but had found herself unable to concentrate.

"If the rest of the house is in the same shape—"

"It is, more or less, except for the bathroom."

"Well, I'll have a look-see around. I noticed last time that in several rooms the woodwork could do with a wash. I tell my customers to call Sonny for that sort of thing. But I'll do the woodwork for you myself."

"Oh, please don't—"

"Got to earn my pay someway. As the fella says, the workman should be worthy of his hire. Now you finish your breakfast."

In the early afternoon Kate climbed the stairs to get a book she had left on her nightstand. Myrtle Thompson called, "Can you come back here? I'm in the empty bedroom. I want to show you something."

Kate went down the hall. In the bedroom Mrs. Thompson stood, scrub cloth in hand, beside a window. "Look at this."

On the window frame's outer edge, at about shoulder height, were smears of coral pink lipstick.

"No wonder everybody missed it, including me," she said. "It's pretty much out of sight, on the window frame's edge like that. You know who I think did it? That Welker girl, Donna Sue. It was just like her to do a slobby thing like that."

"This—this was her room then?"

"Hers and Martin's. And her dressing table was right here by this window. I know because once I took care of her for a week when she had the flu real bad."

Kate felt relief. She had often wondered if they had occupied the room she now used, and she had hated the idea. "I'd have thought she would have preferred one of the front bedrooms, since they have a view."

"Most folks would, but not Donna Sue. She must have liked this room because it was the biggest. As for views, the only view that interested her was her own face in the mirror. Come to think of it, I guess she really wasn't interested in anything except men."

"Oh, Mrs. Thompson! She must have had some other interests."

91

Myrtle Thompson shrugged. "Oh, I heard she liked to cook. But outside of that she didn't do much all day but watch TV and read confession magazines."

"There are two stacks of magazines in the closet across the hall."

"Confession magazines?"

"Yes, and some copies of *The New York Review of Books.*"

Oh, I know where those came from. They've been up in the attic for years. Those highbrow magazines were left here about eight years ago by some college professor. But maybe the confessions were Donna Sue's. I guess the woman Leora hired to get this place ready for you straightened out the attic too. Maybe she planned to take those magazines to the dump and then forgot about it."

She paused. "You want me to get rid of them for you?"

"Oh, no. They're not in my way."

"Just as you say." She looked around the room. "The bed was over against the wall when Donna Sue and Martin had this room. I guess it was taken out for some reason or other and Cousin Leora never had another one put in. Maybe it was because she didn't have any tenants who wanted more than those two bedrooms facing the ocean."

She dipped the cloth in the pail of soapy water at her feet and vigorously attacked the lipstick stain. She thought, slob! And what a filthy little whore. She, a married woman, had gone after Sonny for a while, and him only sixteen at the time!

Well, Sonny had turned out fine. With pride she thought of his panel truck, his window-and-wall-cleaning equipment, his helper. But with Donna Sue's hooks in him, lord knew how he would have turned out if she had stayed alive.

She scrubbed even harder, as if trying to wipe out even the memory of Donna Sue.

At three-thirty, saying she could find nothing more to do, Myrtle Thompson departed, with Kate's check in her worn handbag.

For a while afterward Kate tried to work on a painting, an abstract consisting of swirls of gray and black paint which she had started several days before. Finally she laid down her brush. It was no use. Her mind kept straying from the canvas to that large bedroom down the hall. What had become of its furnishings?

She went down to the kitchen, made out a brief grocery list, and drove into town. When she had left the grocery she put her purchases in the VW and then walked a few yards to Leora Kelso's real estate office in the mall. Through the plate glass she saw the woman at her desk, thumbing through a card catalogue. Kate walked in.

Leora looked up through her harlequin glasses. "Hello, there!"

"Hello. I thought I'd just drop in for a minute or two."

"Glad you did. Have a chair." Then, when Kate had sat down: "Everything going okay?"

"Yes. The house looks much better with curtains up." She paused. "I didn't put any in that big bedroom."

"No reason you should, when you're not using that room."

"Could you tell me why all of its furniture was taken out?"

Leora considered. The New York girl already knew about the murder. There would be no point in evading her question.

"Martin Donnerly wrecked some of it, the night he killed his wife. Oh, not that he admitted tearing up that room or any of the others, anymore than he admitted the murder. But he did it, all right."

"Was that room particularly—"

"Wrecked? Yes. He not only turned dresser drawers upside down and tore up a chair's seat cushion. He ripped the mattress apart with something or other, probably a kitchen knife. Maybe he didn't do that just to make people think the house had been burglarized. Maybe he got some satisfaction out of it, too."

"Satisfaction?"

"Sure. Considering how often she'd cheated on him, it's no wonder he tore up that room worse than the others. It was the room they'd shared."

Kate felt a tightening in the pit of her stomach. Maybe the condition of that room, that bed—his and Donna Sue's marriage bed—*had* been further evidence of his guilt. And yet she still found it hard to believe that it was a killer who had sat beside her on that driftwood log.

"Miss Hillier decided to sell the bedstead and the rest of the things in that room to a junk dealer over in Mockstown. I'll try to get her to replace the furniture if any tenants show up needing more sleeping space. So far none have."

"I see." Kate glanced at her watch. "Almost five! You must be about ready to close up. I'd better go."

She drove home through sunset light, feeling miserably torn between her belief in Martin Donnerly and her fear that such belief was misplaced.

CHAPTER
THIRTEEN

Twice more during the next few days she caught glimpses of Martin in town. But it wasn't until midweek that he again came to the house.

It was April by then, and the weather had turned much warmer. In a white T-shirt and yellow cotton pants she had spent most of the day on the strip of sand in front of the house, sometimes reading, sometimes sketching the sandpipers who raced along the beach, sometimes just staring out at the horizon where an occasional passing freighter left a smudge of dark smoke against the sky. Around six-thirty she was in the kitchen, preparing to mix an omelet for her dinner, when he knocked on the back-door frame.

She looked through the screen. Enough light remained that she could see him out there, one hand holding a canvas carryall. Her heart stepped up its beat. Not speaking, she unlocked the screen door, and he walked in.

He looked at her unsmilingly. "I was out fishing today. A man at the marina in Mockstown loaned me a boat. I caught some mackerel."

"You did?"

"I thought you might want some. It's cleaned, ready to cook."

She said, "If you'll share it with me."

She knew he must have expected, or at least hoped, that she would say that. Nevertheless, the sudden blaze of pleasure in his eyes made her feel a little dizzy.

He set the carryall down on the sinkboard. "I'll broil it. I'm good at that. Have you got some sort of green vegetable?"

"Frozen broccoli."

"That should go fine. Wait just a minute while I go out to the pickup."

When he came back he was carrying a bottle of Chablis. She knew for sure then that he had hoped she would ask him to stay.

While he broiled the fish and cooked the broccoli, she went into the dining room, spread a white polyester cloth, set out inexpensive dinnerware and stainless steel knives and forks. She found herself wishing that she had her mother's Minton china and her grandmother's sterling candelabra and Samuel Kirk flatware.

But when they sat opposite each other at the round table she soon realized that such luxuries wouldn't have helped. Even by candlelight and with a Venetian lace cloth the meal would have been strained. Vaguely she was aware that the freshly caught mackerel was excellent, but she had little appetite for it. They sat there, eating a mouthful now and then, and talking of fishing and sailing and the warm weather, while all the time their eyes, and the tone of their voices, were saying quite different things.

He poured the last of the wine into the two thick tumblers she had set out. When they had drunk the wine,

Kate took the dishes into the kitchen, rinsed them, and placed them in the rack.

Martin said from the doorway, "It's still nice out. Would you like to walk?"

They crossed the rocky strip to the sand, turned to their right. There was no moon, but the sky was thickly strewn with stars, the constellation of the Swan rising in the east, and the Hunter and his Dog descending the western sky. The rollers washed gently onto the beach, their white froth sparked with the pale greenish glow of phosphorescence now and then.

Martin talked about the boatyard. He was waiting for all the necessary permits from the town trustees and from the county. Kate said, in a voice that sounded stilted even to her own ears, that she hoped he wouldn't have to wait long. After that they walked in silence for a while.

Finally she said, "I read that chapter in *Moby Dick*."

"And?"

"It's dazzling. But do you think he really believed that? I mean, that at the very heart of things there is this— this cold horror, this indifference, or worse?"

"Melville is far from being the only writer who has felt that. There was Matthew Arnold, for instance."

"*Dover Beach?*"

He nodded.

"Do you remember it, well enough to say it?"

"Part of it, maybe." He hesitated and then began to speak, in a voice so harsh that she almost felt they were his own words, not those of a man long dead:

> "*—for the world, which seems
> To lie before us like a land of dreams,
> So various, so beautiful, so new,
> Hath really neither joy, nor love, nor light,*

Nor certitude, nor peace, nor help for pain:
And we are here as on a darkling plain
Swept with confused alarms of struggle and flight,
Where ignorant armies clash by night."

Her throat ached with sympathy for him. If only there was some way of reversing time, so that he could again be the young Martin Donnerly, for whom those lines would be just a poem, not a distillation of his own bitter experience.

After a moment she managed to say, "But don't you see?" She halted and faced him. "Even if that's true, even if the world only *seems* like a land of dreams, there are times when it can be very beautiful."

She spread her arms in a gesture that seemed to encompass the star-brilliant sky, the dark ocean, the frothing waves. "Don't you see?"

He looked down at her. "Yes, I see. It can be beautiful, all right, so beautiful that you want to believe it really could be like that, all the way through."

They looked at each other through the starlight. His face was dark, intent. He said, "Kate?"

She swayed toward him. Then she was in his arms, with his mouth warm on hers. She seemed to feel the shock of that kiss all the way through her to the soles of her feet.

He lifted his lips from hers, cradled her face in his hands, kissed her forehead, her throat. She knew now that she was not the only one who had dreamed of a moment like this.

He drew her close against him, pressed her cheek against his shoulder. "I told myself I'd never ask this of you. But now—"

Hands on her upper arms, he held her a little away from him. "Shall we go back to the house?"

"Yes," Kate said.

CHAPTER
FOURTEEN

When she awoke she lay with eyes closed for several moments. She felt happy, without knowing why. Then she remembered.

She and Martin climbing the stairs to this room. His big warm hands undressing her, caressing her body. Her growing need of him. And then the slow climb, so exquisite it was almost painful, to a physical release more complete than any she had ever known.

She opened her eyes. Fully dressed, back turned to her, he stood at the window, silhouetted against the gray morning light. There was something withdrawn in the look of him as he stood there. It filled her with a cold foreboding, and caused her to draw the sheet up to her bare shoulders before she sat up in bed.

"Martin?"

He turned, but did not move toward her. "I was going to leave you a note."

After a moment she asked, in a careful voice, "What did you plan to say in it?"

"That I'm sorry, sorry this happened. It never should have."

She asked, in that same carefully even voice, "Why not?"

He walked over to the bed. "Because you and I aren't casual people. If we were, what happened last night wouldn't matter much, one way or the other. But for us it was important, and so it mustn't happen again."

"Why? *Why?*" She added, in a low, shaken voice, "Can't you see? I think I love you."

"I know. And I love you." He sat down on the bed's edge, near its foot. "But what do you want us to do about it? Get married?"

"Why not?" When he didn't answer she went on swiftly, "We could go to New York. There are shipyards there and in New Jersey. I make enough that we could live on it until you got a good job, the kind a graduate engineer ought to have—"

"Oh, Kate! Use your head. A girl like you, married to an ex-con? A man who has to report regularly to a parole officer? A man who can't even *vote*, for God's sake!"

"And that's not the worst of it." In the dim light his face was bleak. "The worst of it is that you would never be quite sure you hadn't married a murderer. Not absolutely, rock-bottom sure. If you were married to another sort of man, and he did something that angered you, you'd just think, that jerk, or maybe, that bastard. With me, you'd think of where I spent those twelve years, and why. If you became upset enough, you might even throw those years in my face."

She wanted to cry out, no! But she knew he was right. She would never be absolutely sure. How could she or any woman be? Even now she was wondering in some part of her mind if he was choosing to walk away from her because he knew he was guilty.

"Kate, I shouldn't even have come here last night, let alone—I've known all along that I should stay completely away from you, but I kidded myself that it would do no harm to see you once more, talk to you for an hour or so—"

He stood up. "I'm sorry, Kate."

He walked out. She heard his feet descending the stairs. After an interval she heard the sound of his pickup's engine starting up, moving away.

She lay there in the strengthening light, wishing that she had never come to Camelot, never rented this house, never known that Martin Donnerly existed.

But she did know. All she could do now was to keep reminding herself how right he was. Even in New York there would always be the necessity to keep that twelve-year gap in his life concealed. She thought of conversation at some dinner party turning to some movie a few years back, and one of the guests saying to Martin, "What, you didn't see that film? I thought that everyone in the country had."

And, far more serious, there would always be that wretched little doubt in her mind.

She threw back the covers. Get dressed. Have breakfast. Go to work, if not at her easel, then mending a bra strap or waxing the already-waxed kitchen linoleum or *some* damned thing. And after a while this need for him would start to fade.

But it didn't. In fact, it seemed to increase. Two days later it caused her to make a completely unnecessary trip into town. She saw neither Martin nor his pickup. Perhaps he was staying on the other side of the causeway.

The next night she left off trying to watch an old Bette Davis movie on the portable TV she had rented in Mockstown a few days earlier. She went to the telephone

101

nook beneath the staircase. She opened the phonebook which included subscribers in Camelot, Mockstown, and two other small communities. When she turned to the D's, the name Martin Donnerly seemed to leap out at her. After a moment, though, she realized that the book was several years old. The Donnerly listed must be Martin Donnerly, Senior, that man who had disinherited his convict son.

She dialed. After three rings the phone at the other end of the line was lifted. "Hello. David Donnerly speaking." Not at all like Martin's voice. Smooth, self-assured, and slightly drawling.

Feeling ashamed of the impulse which had led her to call, Kate said, "I'm sorry. I have the wrong number," and hung up.

The next night, while she was preparing her hamburger and tomato salad dinner, the phone rang. Heartbeats rapid, she hurried down the hall and lifted the handset from its cradle. "Hello."

"Kate? Is that you, Kate?"

The voice was familiar. Why couldn't she identify it?

"It's me, Kate. Richard."

After a stunned moment she said, "Hello, Richard." Then: "How did you know where to find me?"

"It's taken some doing. When I couldn't get you at your apartment I called your office. They wouldn't tell me anything except that you were taking a leave of absence. It's company policy, I guess, not to give out such information."

He paused. When Kate said nothing, he went on, "I called Maidy Powell, and finally persuaded her to talk. She said you'd gone to a place in North Carolina called Camelot."

He must have been persuasive indeed, Kate reflected. Maidy Powell was one of the bright young legal assistants to Mayor Koch. She was also Kate's best friend, and had taken a very dim view of Richard's behavior after the car accident.

"Kate, I've got to see you."

Urgency in his voice, an urgency she once had longed so much to hear. "Why?"

"We made a mistake."

"We? What mistake, Richard?"

"We should never have let each other go. I realize that more and more. I can't get you out of my mind, Kate. Will you come back here, at least for a day or two?"

When she didn't answer, he said, "I know. By rights, I should come to you, and I will, if necessary. But I really shouldn't leave town. There's this big deal pending with a Chicago brokerage house—"

Again he waited for her to speak and then said, "I want to marry you, Kate. I know that for certain, now."

Only about three months ago what she had wanted most in all the world was to be Mrs. Richard Sedge.

"All right," she said, "I'll come to New York, at least for a day or two."

CHAPTER FIFTEEN

She found New York almost summerlike. On Fifth Avenue, where only weeks before pedestrians had hurried with heads bent against frigid winds sweeping down the broad thoroughfare, people now lounged on the steps of the Metropolitan Museum. The flower beds down the middle of Park Avenue blazed with scarlet and yellow tulips. On the sidewalks, London plane trees had put out their first pale young leaves. And apartment house doormen, who all winter had stood behind heavy plate glass doors, grimly alert to spot unwelcome visitors, or dogs who might lift a leg against plastic shrubbery flanking the entrances, now stood out in the April sunlight, looking almost amiable.

Kate called Richard at his office the first morning after her arrival. They met at the Plaza for dinner. Afterwards they crossed Fifty-ninth Street to where a line of carriages and top-hatted drivers waited for lovers and well-heeled tourists.

The carriage Richard hired drew them along curving Central Park roads. The soft air was fragrant with new grass. Blossoming fruit trees were pale blurs against the darkness. And on either side of the park the apartment buildings, windows glittering, soared like the towers of some magical kingdom.

It was a scene of high romance, lacking only violin music in the background. A year ago, riding through the spring darkness beside Richard, she would have felt a dreamy joy. Now all she felt was discomfort at the thought of what she must say to him.

They went to her apartment. The four rather modest rooms, with their mixture of Bloomingdale's furniture and a few Victorian antiques, seemed luxurious to her after that house on Blackfish Island. They sat on the sofa, small glasses of brandy on the coffee table in front of them.

Richard put his hands on her shoulders, turned her toward him. "Kate, we've got to talk. You've been evading me all evening."

"I know." She looked into his thin, earnest face. It seemed to her incredible that this man once had had the power to shatter her self-esteem far more completely than the accident had shattered her body.

"I realize it may take you time to forgive me. You were right. I really didn't want to marry you then, even though I couldn't bring myself to say so. I'd always planned to marry a girl—well, someone from one of the families I grew up with. And I figured that in time I'd get over you."

His hands tightened on her shoulders. "But it hasn't worked out like that. I've missed you more and more over these past weeks. It's gotten to where my work has begun to suffer. My parents have noticed the change in me too. Last January, I could tell that you were afraid that their acceptance of you would be lukewarm at best, and I suppose it might have been. But now they'll be only too glad to welcome you into the family. I swear it."

Had she ever suffered agonies of anxiety over what two aging people in Boston might think of her?

He went on, "We belong together, Kate. You saw that even before I did." He paused, and then said, "What is it? Is it that you feel you can't forgive me?"

"I've already forgiven you," she said, and found that she had. After all, he had been no villain, seducing an innocent maiden with a promise of marriage and then abandoning her.

"Then what is it, Kate? Why do you seem miles away?"

Because I am, she thought. More than three hundred miles away.

He asked, his voice suddenly harsh, "Have you met someone else?"

"Yes."

"Down there in that little town no one ever heard of? You couldn't have! I looked Camelot up in the atlas. It has a year-round population of less than two thousand."

"Just the same, I met someone."

"Who is he?"

"Martin Donnerly."

"I don't mean just his name! Who is he? What is he?"

"No one you would like. And the fact that I'm in love with a man like him—well, it proves that you were right about me from the first."

"Right about you?"

"Yes, Richard. I would never have been the sort of wife you need. I don't have a sufficient sense of—of propriety, of how a sensible person should conduct her life."

He argued for a while longer. Then he gave up. Looking pale, he nevertheless managed to smile and to

107

wish her good luck before he closed the door behind himself.

After he had gone she sat on the sofa, hands clenched in her lap. She felt grateful to Richard for having asked her to come back here. Seeing him had erased her last doubt about what she wanted to do. She wanted to marry Martin.

And the fear that both she and Martin felt, the fear that she would never be entirely sure that he had not fired that shotgun? She saw now that there was one way, and only one way, by which that fear might be erased.

Someone had killed Martin's wife. If Martin had not, then someone else was guilty. She knew the chance was slim indeed that the person could be found, especially at this late date. Nevertheless, she was going to try her damnedest, because otherwise she and Martin would live out their separate lives, never knowing what the years might have brought the two of them.

She went into her bedroom and began to pack, so that she could start driving south the first thing in the morning.

CHAPTER
SIXTEEN

She made excellent time on the trip south. It was still full
daylight when she drove down Mockstown's main street,
past the small shops and the one department store, past
the McDonald's and the two gas stations on opposite
corners and the movie theater which, unlike the one in the
village on Blackfish Island, was open every night of the
week.

Because it offered a wider choice than the Camelot
grocery, Kate stopped at the Mockstown A&P. Then she
drove across the causeway with its broken asphalt and
rusting side rails. Sunset pink and gold were touching the
water now and dyeing the white undersides of wheeling
gulls.

She left her car in the little garage and, carrying two
bags of groceries, walked to the house. She set down the
bags long enough to unlock the back door and then went
inside.

Smell of lemon-scented furniture polish. Of course.
This was a Friday. Mrs. Thompson had been here, using
her own keys to get in.

She put the bags down on the sinkboard, switched on the light, and began to put her purchases away in cupboards and the refrigerator.

It began to steal over her, that sense that she was not alone in this house. Soon it became so strong that she began to wonder if Myrtle Thompson was still here, despite the fact that her old sedan had not been standing beside the garage. At last, feeling a little foolish, she went down the hall to the foot of the stairs and, looking up, called the woman's name.

No answer. No movement at the top of the stairs.

Already that odd feeling had begun to fade. She returned to the kitchen, finished putting away the groceries, and went out to get her suitcase. She carried it up to her bedroom, placed it on the bed, and then, instead of starting to unpack, walked over to the window and looked out.

The sunset had faded. Below the window the wide swathe of rounded stones, reflecting what light was left, gleamed dully. Beyond the rocks was the narrower strip of sand and then the fringe of low white rollers and then the flat plane of the Atlantic, no longer blue but battleship gray.

She thought of awakening her first night in this house and crossing to this window and seeing Darleen Mae down there. She had become sure that it had to have been Donna Sue's retarded sister. Neither in Camelot or Mockstown or anywhere in between had she seen anyone who even resembled the girl who had stood down there on that strip of sand, classic face upturned to the cold moonlight.

She was Martin's sister-in-law. Odd to think of her as that, but she was, or at least had been. And the next morning after Kate had seen her Martin himself had come here. Coincidence? Perhaps. But it could be that the girl, hearing of Martin's release from prison, had for some reason felt compelled to cross the causeway and wander past this house.

Had she visited this house often while her sister was alive? Kate tried to imagine them together. Donna Sue, the elder by a few minutes, lazy and sluttish and, in Chadwick Garner's phrase, completely amoral. Darleen Mae, doomed to live out her life as a young child. And both of them with that perfect face, framed in pale yellow hair.

Yes, Kate decided, Donna Sue might have welcomed visits from her retarded twin. She would have been able to confide to Darleen Mae almost anything she chose, secure in the knowledge that her sister would not comprehend.

Perhaps she would mention Darleen Mae to Martin the next time she saw him.

If she saw him. For all she knew, he had decided to give up the boatyard idea and go away someplace.

Thrusting the unbearable idea from her, she walked over to the bed and began to unpack her suitcase. When she had finished she went down to the kitchen, prepared herself a ground lamb patty and a green salad, and ate it under the dining room's fake Tiffany chandelier. Tired from the drive down from New York, she cleared the table and then went up to bed almost immediately.

Her sleep was restless. In her dreams uninvited visitors invaded the house. She could not tell what they looked like because their features kept changing, like faces seen by wavering candlelight. But she somehow knew that they were members of the Welker family, and that she was afraid of them.

111

Twice she awoke in the darkness. Once, during the Welker dream, when one of the fluid-featured people, a woman, reached out to touch her, a part of her dreaming mind said, "I don't have to stand this. It isn't real. Wake up!" and she did.

The second time, an unmeasured interval later, she awoke with a sense that there had been sounds of stealthy movement on the lower floor. For perhaps five minutes she lay awake and rigid. Then she went back to sleep.

Over breakfast the next morning she made a resolve. Without delay she was going to embark upon the perhaps impossible task of proving that someone other than Martin had shot his wife to death in this house one hot night a dozen summers ago. And her first step was going to be to learn all she could about his wife's family.

If nothing else, seeing them in the flesh would keep her from spending nights like the last one. Once she knew what they actually looked like, they would no longer troop through her dreams with faces that dissolved and reformed even as she looked at them. To her they would become just people, ignorant and feckless and perhaps even criminal, but still recognizable human beings.

She drove into the village and found a parking place a few doors from the *Clarion*. As before Chadwick Garner sat in his front office, feet on his desk, newspaper in his hands. Today though it was not *The New York Times* but *Barron's Weekly*.

He smiled at sight of her and got to his feet. "Great to see you! I was just thinking of phoning you to see if you were back from New York. I figured your trip might make a small news item."

"How did you know I'd gone to New York?"

112

"I forget who—Oh, yes. It was Leora Kelso."

She had told Myrtle Thompson she was going to New York for a few days, and Mrs. Thompson obviously had told her cousin. "It was just a—a business trip. Nothing newsworthy. I'm afraid I've come to get information, not give it."

"What this time?"

"Orren Welker."

He looked at her, considering. Could it be that the girl had some wild idea that if she poked around in the past vigorously enough she could find some way of clearing Martin Donnerly of that twelve-year-old murder charge?

"You must mean that you want to find out more about that armored truck robbery."

"Yes. If I could look at your file copies—"

"Sure."

They went back through the pressroom. It was empty today, and the flatbed press stood silent. "We're fresh out of job printing. And the *Clarion* doesn't go to press until Tuesday."

In the back room he switched on the drop light above the long table. He brought out a tall volume from the cubbyhole, spread it out on the table, leafed through it. "Here you are. Story starts with the holdup. I didn't know local people were mixed up in it when I first ran the story. I gave it space in the August issue just because the robbery took place only about forty miles from here."

He left her. She bent over the outspread pages. On a summer morning fifteen years ago, according to the column of newsprint, two young men had crouched in the bushes on either side of a road in Lethener County, North Carolina. Armed with hand grenades and a submachine gun, they had waited for an armored truck which regularly

113

carried payroll money from a Wilmington bank to an electronics factory about fifteen miles away in the country.

The truck appeared and the two robbers attacked. Under the first salvo, the driver ran the truck up onto the bank, where it stalled. But neither the driver nor the man beside him had been hit. They fought back with their own automatic weapons and managed to kill one of the attackers. When the brief but fierce fight was over, the truck driver also lay dead near his mortally wounded assistant.

The second attacker had disappeared, along with two gray denim bags holding more than a hundred thousand dollars in unmarked bills.

By the time the local police arrived, summoned by the occupants of a farmhouse a half-mile down the road, the driver's assistant was near death. Nevertheless, he managed to give the police a description of the man who had disappeared.

Kate found nothing about the robbery in the next two issues of the *Clarion*, but the rest of the story occupied most of the August thirty-first issue. Working from the description furnished by the truck driver's dying assistant, the police had narrowed down the suspects to a few men, among them Orren Welker, 22, a man with a record of several previous arrests. As the police car drove onto the Welker family property in a rural area near Mockstown, Orren broke out of the house and ran in among the pine trees. The police shouted for him to halt. Instead he wheeled and fired a pistol at them. They shot him dead.

The next issue carried two items about the Welker case. Orren's funeral had been held. And the authorities, after searching the Welker property for more than a week and questioning every member of the family, had decided that Orren must have hidden the money somewhere else.

Kate looked through several more issues, but there was no further mention of the armored car robbery.

She closed the volume, then stared unseeingly at the photo of Chad Garner and the senator. Could it be, she was thinking, that the idea advanced by Martin's lawyer—an idea rejected by the jury—actually had been the true explanation of Donna Sue's death?

Suppose the police had not searched the Welker property thoroughly enough. Or suppose Orren had hidden the money, with his family's knowledge, several miles away from the house. The Welkers would not dare start spending it until several years had passed. Thus the money was probably still in its hiding place when, more than two years after the robbery, Donna Sue Welker had married Martin Donnerly and moved with him into the Hillier house.

But after that had the Welkers become afraid, for one reason or another, that the money might be discovered? Had they decided that it would be safer in Donna Sue's house, over on the island? Perhaps. And then could it be that someone else—perhaps the same person they had feared might find the original hiding place—had learned that the money was in the Hillier house? He had come there that hot summer night while Martin, furious and heartsick, had driven aimlessly over the countryside. Had Donna Sue refused to tell this unknown person where the money was? Had he shot her, either in a rage or quite calmly, and then proceeded to ransack the house?

Pulse rapid now, Kate thought, yes, that could have been it. But how to prove it, how to find that man—or woman—who had killed Donna Sue and then walked away, leaving her young husband to pay for the crime with twelve years of his life?

She carried the tall volume into the cubbyhole and placed it in a vacant spot on one of the shelves. Then she walked through the pressroom into the front office. Garner stood up. "Finished?"

"Unless there's more about what became of that payroll money."

"There isn't. It's still a mystery."

After a moment she said, "I remember reading the last time I was here that Martin Donnerly's lawyer suggested that the money might have been hidden in the Hillier house. He said that perhaps Donna Sue had been killed by someone looking for it."

He smiled. "That was a lawyerly ploy, a red herring, if you like. Of course, it could have possibly been true. Almost anything is possible." He paused. "Are you thinking of going on a treasure hunt?"

"In the Hillier house, you mean? The idea hadn't occurred to me."

No, he thought, she was after something she regarded as much more important than money. "I don't think you'd have much chance of finding it, even if it had been there once. The police combed the house thoroughly. And a lot of people have lived there since."

"I know."

He said, after a moment, "Not thinking of paying a call on the Welkers, are you?"

She said carefully, "They do sound—interesting."

"To a sociologist, perhaps. They wouldn't be interesting to you. They're not something out of *Li'l Abner*. And they're not rascally but amusing like the people in *Tobacco Road*. They're sly and mean and violent."

116

After a moment she said enigmatically, "Don't worry."
Then: "Mr. Garner?"

"Don't call me that. It makes me feel like a senior citizen. Call me Chad."

"All right. And I'm Kate. What I was going to ask is, have you ever heard people say there was something—odd about the Hillier house?"

He looked at her quizzically. "You mean haunted?"

"Yes, I suppose I do."

"Well, all I've ever heard along that line is that Leora Kelso has had trouble keeping tenants. But I think that the explanation of that is less likely to be ghosts than poor insulation. I hear that the place can be Siberia in the winter and Calcutta in the summer. Anyway, ghosts can't hurt you. People like the Welkers can. Remember that."

"All right." She smiled. "Goodbye."

CHAPTER SEVENTEEN

Outside in the hazy sunlight Kate took a few steps and then stopped short. Martin had just emerged from the bank onto the opposite sidewalk. He stepped off the curb, caught sight of her, hesitated. Then he crossed the street. He said, unsmiling, "I hear you've been away."

"Yes. I went to New York." She paused, but he didn't speak, and so she went on deliberately, "A man called me up and suggested we see each other again, and so I went up there."

Martin still didn't speak.

Kate said, "He'd decided he wanted to marry me."

His face paled slightly under its tan, but his voice remained even. "What did you tell him?"

"I said no."

She saw a betraying look of pleasure in his eyes. Nevertheless he said in that same tone, "Is he a nice guy?"

"Very. Reliable, successful, good family, the works."

"Then it wasn't very smart of you to turn him down, was it?"

She didn't answer that. Instead she said, after a moment, "How is the boatyard coming along?"

119

"Slowly. I'm going up to Baltimore tomorrow to look at some used equipment. I'll be gone for several days." He paused and then burst out, "Why don't you go back where you belong? What good can you do either of us, hanging around here?"

She said, "Maybe I will go, in a week or so. But not right now."

"Kate, I'm not going to change my mind. It would never work. All I could do is spoil your life. If it hadn't been for those twelve years, you and I would have been great together. But the twelve years did happen, and they changed me in ways you could never understand, ways I wouldn't *want* you to understand. So for God's sake, go away."

He walked past her and got into the blue truck parked a few yards away at the curb. She watched him make a U-turn and then drive off in the direction of the causeway. Still with that set look, she got into the VW. What was it she had planned to buy? Oh, yes. Toothpaste and shampoo. She started the car and drove to the shopping mall.

Standing behind his plateglass window, Chadwick Garner had observed the meeting between Kate and Martin Donnerly. It had been obvious, from the look on his face and from his body language—the set of his almost burly shoulders, the swiftness of his stride as he walked toward the pickup—that he wanted to remain aloof from her. It was equally obvious that she was stubbornly hanging in there. Damn fool girl! Couldn't she see that he was doing her a favor?

Again Garner thought of asking her to lunch or dinner in the hope that he could talk some sense into her. But no. She might very well resent his interference, and resentment might actually strengthen her resolve to stay here.

120

Besides, the chances that she could dredge up any new information about a twelve-year-old murder were miniscule indeed. Sooner or later she would become discouraged and go back to New York.

There was still another reason why he should concern himself as little as possible, a reason he hadn't confided even to his fiancée. Of late he had been having chest pains, not severe, but naggingly frequent. Several times in the night he had awakened abruptly, unable to get his breath. No, if he wanted to marry Stephanie, wanted to run for Congress—and he did want to, so bad he could taste it—then he had better not put himself to any except unavoidable strains.

He turned, sat down at his desk, and resumed his reading of *Barron's Weekly.*

Vanessa Weyant, behind the bank's big front window, also had observed the meeting between Martin and that Kiligrew girl. Now she sat at her desk, ostensibly reading the bank examiner's recent report, but in fact not even seeing the blocks of figures.

Instead she was seeing her bedroom on a summer afternoon fifteen years in the past. Light had been filtering through Venetian blinds to gleam on Martin's bare shoulders as he lay on the bed beside her. Leaning over her, he had gathered her close and covered her mouth with his. All these years later the memory of that kiss brought a tingling sensation to her lips.

He had been eighteen and on vacation from college. She had been twenty-four, living with her widowed father in the Weyant house. As befitted a bank president's house, it was by far the finest in the community, a white frame colonial situated on the southern tip of the island, its back turned to the village. There was even a swimming pool, the only one on Blackfish Island.

Her father had gone to Wilmington that Saturday, leaving her alone in the house except for Matty Grimes. For as long as Vanessa could remember, Matty had worked for the Weyants. Since the death of Vanessa's mother five years before, she had been in sole charge of the household.

That afternoon Vanessa had telephoned Weber's Garage, where Martin had a summer job. She'd asked to speak to him. "Martin, my car won't start. Can you come here and fix it?"

"I don't know, Miss Weyant. We're pretty busy. I don't think the boss would—"

"You tell Ed Webster he can charge double for your time. Tell him to put it on my bill."

Half an hour later Martin came rattling up the drive in the old Chevrolet he had driven that summer. Vanessa, lying bikini-clad beside the pool, had put on a thigh-length white terry robe and accompanied Martin into the shadowy triple garage. He lifted the hood of her red MG and within minutes found and reattached the wire she had loosened before she phoned him. He got into the car, switched on the ignition, and said above the engine's roar, "That does it."

He got out of the car. Vanessa said, "Would you like a drink?"

They looked at each other through the garage's dim light. The suddenly bedazzled expression on his young face told her that he had understood. "Sure," he said, in a constrained voice.

They went into the house. In the big living room with

its drawn blinds and softly humming air conditioner she mixed bourbon and water at the four-stool bar in one corner, added ice. They sat on the sofa, saying almost nothing. She could hear distant sounds from the kitchen. Matty, preparing dinner. Always a noisy cook, given to banging pots and pans around, she had become noisier as she had become deafer.

Because of that deafness, Matty might not even be aware that Martin was on the premises. Anyway, Vanessa felt too reckless to care.

She got up, set down her empty glass. Martin followed her out of the room and up the stairs.

That was all she'd ever had of him, those two hours in her bedroom. Although she hadn't known it at the time, he already had met Donna Sue Welker, that piece of trash who'd come to work at the diner. Soon he was blind to everyone and everything except Donna Sue.

Each summer when he came home from college Vanessa had hoped that he would have outgrown his interest in that tacky little bitch. Instead, he finally had married her. .

Well, she had been dead a long time now. When Martin had come back from prison and approached the bank for a loan, Vanessa had been sure that everything would be different now. Those years in prison had aged him. On the other hand, she had kept herself trim and young-looking. Their age difference, never important to her, seemed even less so now. She would help him realize that old, stubbornly held dream of building a boatyard. Soon they would marry—

But now here was that Kiligrew girl. No slut like Donna Sue, but well educated and well bred. And what-

123

ever the relationship between herself and Martin, she was determined to hold onto it. The look on her face as they talked had made that plain.

True, Martin had walked away from her. But that did not mean that he was not attracted to her. He was strongly attracted. That fact too had been obvious as they faced each other.

How long would he hold out against that attraction?

Get rid of her, Vanessa thought. There were ways. The bank held mortgages on several of old Mrs. Hillier's properties. She could be pressured into evicting her latest tenant.

True, there were plenty of vacancies in Camelot this time of year. But nearly all of them were handled by Leora Kelso, and the bank could pressure Leora. At any time it could call in the loan Leora had taken out in order to build a rental apartment above her garage two years ago.

A sudden thought struck Vanessa. The Kiligrew girl might rent a place in Mockstown. The bank didn't wield nearly as much influence beyond the other end of the causeway.

All right, Vanessa thought. Then she'd have to be gotten rid of some other way.

When she left her car in the cramped garage Kate did not go into the house. Instead she walked through the late morning sunlight to the tiny scrap of front yard with its daffodils, some now in bloom, rising above grass that was taking on the first tinge of green.

Yes, there was that rusty charm bracelet just where she had dropped it. She picked it up and carried it into the house.

CHAPTER
EIGHTEEN

The scraggly pines crowded close to the road, cutting off whatever breeze might have been stirring. Feeling perspiration on her forehead, Kate wanted to drive faster, but dared not. The narrow road, little more than a track, was filled with potholes.

She had awakened that morning to find the day sunless but sultry, perhaps offering a foretaste of the southern July and August. The gray sea, which gleamed dully here and there when sunlight filtered through thin spots in the cloud cover, had an oily look. The low rollers moving toward shore seemed almost sluggish.

As she prepared breakfast, Kate too felt lethargic. One reason might have been the weather. An even stronger one, she realized, was her conversation with Chad Garner. Despite her resolve to visit the Welkers as soon as possible, his warning words about them had shaken her.

She kept putting off her departure. She manicured her nails. She shampooed her hair and then sat on the front step, drying it with a towel. It was late enough by then that she decided she might as well have lunch before setting out. Thus it was almost two o'clock by the time she drove across the causeway's lumpy asphalt.

At the larger of Mockstown's two gas stations she had the VW's tank filled. Then she asked the attendant, "Do you know some people named Welker?"

A thin, sandy-haired man, he looked at her curiously. "Roy and Bonnie Welker? Sure, I know them."

"Could you tell me how to get to their place?"

He nodded. "Take the highway out of town for a couple of miles, then turn right onto the county road. After about five miles you'll see an old water tower, all stove in. Maybe a quarter of a mile beyond it you'll see a dirt road leading to your right through the woods. It's only about four miles long. The Welker place is clean at the end of it."

"Thank you."

"You some kind of reporter?"

"No. Why?"

"A reporter went there a couple of years ago. He was doing some sort of magazine piece about how all over the country there's stolen money that's never been accounted for. Big money, from bank robberies and such." He paused. "I guess maybe you heard that years back the cops tried to arrest the oldest Welker boy for an armored car robbery. They had to shoot him dead."

She said carefully, "I think I've heard something about it." Then, after a moment: "Do you know when and where the reporter's story was printed?"

"Can't say it ever was. All I know is that a couple of days after he went to the Welker's place he was found in his car beside the county highway, beat up bad. He said that two guys with stockings pulled over their faces had run him off the highway and then gone at him with tire irons."

Clasping the wheel with hands that felt suddenly cold, Kate asked, "Did they ever find out who did it?"

"No. I guess the cops couldn't get enough evidence to make an arrest. Everybody had an idea who did it, though."

Well, she'd realized even before this that she would have to be very careful. The trick would be to find out as much as she could without making the Welkers angry or suspicious.

The attendant racked up the gasoline hose, took her twenty-dollar bill, came back with change. "You going out to the Welker's place now?"

"I might." Before he could ask another question she started the engine and drove away.

Now, half an hour later, she maneuvered the little car cautiously along the bumpy road that led east from the collapsed water tower. Now and then she saw shanties among the trees. Some were of frame, some of rusting corrugated metal, some of tar paper, but without exception they had at least one stripped-down car body in their front yards. She saw only a few people, a woman hanging clothes beside her corrugated house and, about a half-mile farther on, three tow-headed children jumping up and down on an old automobile seat beside a tar paper shack. Several times dogs ran out, gave noisy chase to the VW for a few seconds, and then trotted back toward their homes.

She turned a curve. Up ahead the road ended in a roughly semi-circular clearing of bare earth. A small frame house stood in the center of the clearing. Much of the brown paint on its clapboards had peeled away, giving it a leprous look. A sagging porch stretched across the front of the house. On it sat a man, his feet in worn ankle boots up

127

on the railing. On the other side of the screen door, farther back toward the front wall of the house, a woman sat in another straight chair, her hands folded in her lap.

As she drove into the clearing Kate heard a thudding sound, followed by the clang of metal against metal. It wasn't until she stopped her car that she saw the source of the sound. To her left, a few feet from a car's rusting body, two men were pitching horseshoes. Almost with disbelief she saw that they both wore overalls. The thought of Al Capp's characters crossed her mind, followed immediately by the memory of Chad Garner's words: "They're not something out of Li'l Abner.... They're sly and mean and violent."

The two men stopped their play to watch her switch off the VW's engine. A swift glance from the corner of her eye told her that obviously they were brothers, both of them tall and dark and thin. The one she took to be the elder was about thirty, the other one perhaps a year younger.

Uncomfortably aware of their flat, dark stare, Kate got out of the car and closed its door. She called to the motionless figures on the porch, "Mr. and Mrs. Welker?"

It was the woman who finally answered. Two of her upper front teeth, Kate noticed, were missing. "That's right. I'm Bonnie Welker, and there's my husband, Roy. Over there's our two boys, Elvin and Earl." She paused. "Who might you be?"

"My name's Kate Kiligrew." Nervousness made her voice sound stilted. "I'm staying over in Camelot in a house that belongs to a Miss Hillier."

The woman said nothing. Her wispy gray hair framed a sunbrowned, much-wrinkled face set with small blue eyes. Her body appeared to be shapeless beneath a loose, quite new-looking red-and-white print dress of some sleazy material. Her feet, bare on this warm day, had overlapping big toes, their nails black-rimmed. It was hard to imagine that she had been attractive even in her youth. Now she made the name Bonnie seem a derisively cruel misnomer.

Kate threw a swift glance at Roy Welker. Clad in brown pants and a sleeveless undershirt, he looked even fatter than his wife, his freckled bare arms thick, his belly bulging over his belt. Strange to think that these two had produced a kind of backwoods Helen of Troy, a girl whose beauty had troubled many and eventually brought disaster to herself.

Kate said, into the silence, "I heard your daughter once lived in the Hillier house."

Bonnie's wrinkled features squeezed themselves together, as if she were about to burst into tears. "My baby got *kilt* in that house."

The shorter of the two young men—Elvin? Earl?— said, "Her husband kilt her."

As she met his level dark stare, Kate thought of the reporter who had been found battered and bloody in his car at the roadside.

Almost certainly, just by coming here, she had aroused their suspicion, and that was unfortunate. But if she left now, she would have put herself in danger for nothing. Better to try to glean some additional bit of information, if she could.

She said, "Yes, I heard that. But I also heard that some people think that somebody else did it."

He didn't answer. In the silence Kate heard the barking of a distant dog and the raucous cry of a bluejay

129

somewhere nearby in the pine woods. She persisted, "I heard a story that maybe her death had something to do with a payroll robbery—"

"Orren didn't steal that money!" Bonnie cried. "My boy got mixed up with bad company for a while, but he was never near that truck! The law had always been down on us Welkers, that's all. They come out here looking for him, and Orren got scared and run off through the trees, and they shot him dead!"

No mention of Orren's firing on the police.

Kate said, "If your son got mixed up in bad company, maybe it was some friend of his who did the robbery."

Sniffling, Bonnie didn't answer.

"Anyway, I heard that whoever did it might have hid the money in the Hillier house. And when he came to get it, he and your daughter had some kind of a quarrel, and he—he shot her."

Even though she didn't look at the Welker brothers, she was very much aware of them standing a few feet away from her. Could one of them have blasted Donna Sue, his own sister, with a shotgun? It was hard to imagine. But perhaps, as Chad Garner had implied, people like the Welkers were capable of almost anything.

"Wait a minute!" Bonnie Welker's voice was no longer tearful, but cold and hard. "Why're you so interested? Why'd you come here, anyway?"

"Oh, I almost forgot." Kate unfastened the flap of her shoulder bag, reached inside. "I found this in the front yard of the Hillier house."

She moved a little way up the porch steps, held out her hand. "I could tell it had been there for a long time, so I thought it might have belonged to your daughter."

Bonnie leaned forward, took the charm bracelet, and looked at it lying on her dirt-streaked palm. She had never seen it in her life before. "Yes, that was my baby's," she said tearfully, and dropped it into the pocket of her tentlike garment.

She had never liked Donna Sue, she reflected, not even when she was real little. Cross her anyway at all, and she'd start howling and kicking and biting. And when she got older, she'd flaunt herself before anything in pants. No wonder that even her own daddy would look at her in a certain way. Bonnie had seen him do it, dozens of times.

Now Darleen Mae was different. Never sassed back, never gave a mite of trouble, and did as she was told, or anyway near as she could. Sure, she'd never been right in the head. But Bonnie still was glad that Darleen Mae wasn't the twin that got shot.

Kate said, "I'm glad I was able to give you your daughter's bracelet. Well, I suppose I'd better be going."

"Wait a minute." Roy Welker spoke for the first time. His small brown eyes, more intelligent than his wife's, were bright with suspicion. "You make the trip from Camelot just to bring us that gimcrackery thing?"

"Oh, no. For several days I've been sort of exploring the countryside. Last night I decided to drive around here. I brought the bracelet just on the chance I could find out where you lived. A man in the filling station in Mockstown told me how to find you."

She added swiftly, "Well, goodbye."

Bonnie sniffled. No one else made a sound. Kate got into the VW, backed, and drove out of the clearing.

The day was fading. It was darker along the road now, and the air seemed even closer than before. Despite the dangerous potholes in the narrow road, she fed the little car more gas. It wasn't just because of the road's hot gloom that she wanted to get back on the county road as soon as possible. It was because of the Welker brothers. She'd seen no car back there except that rusting wreck. But surely there must be some sort of vehicle on the premises, probably a four-wheel drive capable of making good time even on a road as rough as this one. Ears straining for the sound of another engine, she thought of them back there a hundred yards or so—

She turned a curve. There ahead of her, walking in the roadside ditch, was a slender figure in a black-and-white checked shirt and worn blue jeans, with pale, silky-looking hair falling below her shoulders. Kate's pulse leaped. She slowed the car, stopped.

"Darleen Mae?"

The girl had halted. Luminous gray eyes wide set in a classically lovely face. A sweet, utterly guileless smile. Kate said, "You are Darleen Mae, aren't you?"

The girl nodded.

Kate swung the door back. "Would you like a ride?" She felt doubly fortunate in encountering Darleen Mae. Now she would not only have a chance to talk to Donna Sue's brain-damaged twin, it was also reasonable to think that if the two young Welkers were indeed somewhere back along this road, the presence of their sister might have a restraining effect upon them.

"Yes." Darleen Mae said and got into the car.

Kate drove on. From the corner of her eye she looked at the exquisite profile. Darleen Mae was smiling with the uncomplicated pleasure of a four-year-old in a swing. With a sense of shock Kate realized that in actuality her passenger was several years older than herself.

Kate asked, "Where were you going?"

"The road."

She must mean the county road, Kate realized after a moment. She asked, "Do you go lots of places?"

Darleen Mae turned that seraphic smile toward her. "Oh, yes. I go all over."

With dismay Kate realized that probably that was true. Probably, with little more concern than if she had been a cat or a dog, the Welkers allowed this childlike creature to roam wherever she chose.

"Do you ever cross the causeway to Blackfish Island?"

"Blackfish. I've been there."

"Were you over there one night less than a month ago?"

As if she'd been reminded of her inadequacy, a troubled look came into the beautiful gray eyes. "I don't remember."

Kate said, gently persistent, "You don't remember walking past the house where Donna Sue used to live?"

"Donna Sue. I remember Donna Sue. She was good to me. She lived in a big house. She let me stay with her all day sometimes."

It was the first time Kate had heard anyone speak well of Donna Sue.

"But that was years ago. You don't remember being on Blackfish Island one night recently?"

Darleen Mae shook her head.

Kate listened. Still no sound of a pursuing vehicle. She turned another curve. Ahead was the county road,

133

with a car and house trailer moving along it. She stopped the VW.

"It must be almost your supper time. Don't you think you'd better go home?"

"Yes."

Docilely Darleen Mae got out, smiled at Kate once more, and started back up the rutted road.

CHAPTER
NINETEEN

Kate spent a troubled night. Several times she came awake abruptly, not knowing what had aroused her. Some dream which had faded before her conscious mind could grasp it? Or some sound? She thought of the Welker brothers, crouched at a rear window, cutting the locked screen—

After minutes of straining her ears and hearing no sound except the wash of waves, she would fall asleep, only to awaken again an unmeasured interval later.

In the morning, right after breakfast, she called Chief Bosley. "You mentioned a locksmith friend of yours—"

"That's right. Jed Phillips. You decided to take my advice?"

"In a way. I mean, the doors seem secure enough to me. They have thumb latches as well as locks. It's the windows that worry me. I don't imagine your friend has any window alarms, but perhaps he could tell me where I—"

"You're wrong, little lady. Jed's got window alarms. We got no way here in Camelot of wiring them into police headquarters, but he's got alarms that will make one hell of a racket if anyone tries to break in."

"Really? I figured that in a community this small—"

"Jed's been stuck with more than a dozen alarms for the past five years. You know the Weyants, run the bank?"

"Yes. At least I know Miss Weyant."

"Well, five years ago old man Weyant decided to put window alarms on that big house of his. Jed ordered the alarms, but then Weyant decided he'd need them only on the ground floor. He wouldn't pay for the extra alarms, and the manufacturer wouldn't take them back, so Jed's been stuck with them."

"Well, I've counted the windows on the ground floor here. There are ten of them. Do you think Mr. Phillips would sort of rent them to me? I mean, I'd pay him for his time, and whatever above that he considered fair, and then he could take them back when I give up the house."

"You leave that to me. I'll talk him into it. We'll be there around ten o'clock, say."

"Oh, no! I wouldn't dream of taking you away from your office. If you'll just call Mr. Phillips for me—"

"My deputy can handle everything here," he said, and hung up.

They arrived a few minutes after ten, the locksmith in a yellow panel truck, Bosley in Camelot's one and only police car. Bosley was sprucely uniformed in khaki with a black tie knotted beneath his Adam's apple. His companion wore blue overalls. A pleasant, rather shy man, with blue eyes behind horn-rimmed glasses and a glistening bald head, Jed Phillips moved from window to window, trailed by Kate and the police chief. At last, saying that he couldn't forsee any problems, he went out the back door to get the alarms from his truck.

Kate said, "If you'll excuse me now." She left the kitchen and started back along the hall toward the stairs.

Catching up with her, Bosley said, "Going upstairs? I'll go with you, make sure the windows up there'll be okay."

"No!" Kate cried. Then, embarrassed by her own vehemence: "I mean, I'm sure no one can break into the upstairs windows. There are no trees close by, and that flimsy drain pipe wouldn't support anyone's weight. Besides, I planned to work."

She added lamely, "If you'd like, please make yourself a cup of coffee. There's a jar of instant in the refrigerator."

Standing in the hall, Chief Bosley watched her climb the stairs. Uppity bitch, he thought.

How he hated women! Either they looked down their noses at you, like this one. Or they were whining scarecrows like his wife. Or they were teasing little whores like Donna Sue Welker.

He thought of the time he'd caught her and some of her friends in one of the empty summer cottages. Donna Sue must have been about seventeen then. They'd broken into the place, bringing several six packs with them. They'd found some candles and lit them, and were sitting around the kitchen giggling and drinking when he used a skeleton key on the back door and walked in on them.

Except for Donna Sue they'd all looked scared, too scared to say anything, let alone try to run. Donna Sue, though, had said, sounding respectful but not in the least frightened, "Chief Bosley, could I talk to you in the next room?"

In the boxlike little living room she turned to him,

her face dimly illuminated by the candlelight from the kitchen. She no longer looked respectful. "You be nice to us, Chief, and I'll be nice to you. How about meeting me right here tomorrow night at eight o'clock?"

He'd let the kids go. The next night he'd waited in the unlighted cottage until about ten, but she hadn't shown. When he ran into her on the street several days later she'd said her folks had locked her in the house that night because she'd had a big fight with them. "But," she'd added, "how about meeting me tonight, same place?"

That night he waited an hour for her, then left.

Twice more that summer she'd promised to meet him, but hadn't. He'd decided to try to forget the whole thing.

Now he turned and walked into the room with the green manteled fireplace. He stood in its doorway and thought of how she'd looked lying there, after taking a blast from a double-barreled shotgun in her face and chest. There hadn't been much left then to torment a man.

Upstairs, Kate gave up work on a new painting, a seascape with sandpipers in the foreground. She went to her bedroom, lay down on the bed, and tried to read a paperback, Isak Dinesen's *Seven Gothic Tales*, which she'd bought in a stationery store in Mockstown several days before. From the lower floor came the sound of Jed Phillips's labors, window sashes raised and lowered, a drill's whine, and now and then the banging of a hammer. After a while there was another sound, an engine starting up and moving away. She knew it must be the chief's car rather than the panel truck, because the sounds from the ground floor continued. She felt relieved that Bosley was out of the house.

138

She glanced at her watch. Well past noon. She hoped the locksmith would finish before long. By now she had expected to be on the other side of the causeway, driving toward the Donnerly house.

She felt a need to see it, that house where Martin had been born and raised, that house which Martin Donnerly, senior, had left, not to his convict older son, but to his younger one.

And if she were to drive past the place she wanted it to be before Martin returned from Baltimore. She didn't want to risk encountering him. She shrank from the thought that he would be sure to believe that it was her determined pursuit of him, rather than a need to see where he had grown up, that had caused her to drive past his house.

The sounds on the first floor ceased. After a few moments Jed Phillips called up the stairs, "Lady?"

"Yes?"

"I've finished."

"Thank you, Mr. Phillips. I'll settle up with you."

She took her checkbook from her handbag and descended the stairs.

CHAPTER
TWENTY

Because it was so late, she decided to have lunch before going to the mainland. Thus it was a little after two when she drove through Mockstown. At the end of its main street she turned right. No need to ask for directions. In the phone book the Donnerly address was given as County Road Number Seven. She had looked that road up on the map in her glove compartment and seen that Number Seven branched off the state highway about five miles north of Mockstown.

She left the well-traveled highway for the less crowded county road. Here fields of what she thought might be tobacco—dark green plants, large-leaved and more than knee high—separated big houses set far back on wide lawns. But she saw that this was not *Gone With The Wind* country, at least not anymore. Most of the houses appeared to have been built in this century. Some of them, with glass walls and with roofs on several levels, reminded her of the ultra-modern houses that during the past decade had sprung up among the potato fields on eastern Long Island.

She came to a broad pasture, enclosed by a split rail fence, where several horses grazed and two colts, tails flying, raced across the grass. Up ahead, its roof rising above trees, was what looked like an antebellum house. She drove slowly and admiringly past, looking at the sweep of graveled drive, the broad veranda with its white pillars, the red brick facade. She was several yards beyond the brick pillars flanking the drive when it registered upon her mind that there had been a brass plate affixed to one of them.

She stopped, backed up. Yes, the plate said, "Donnerly." She looked at the house with even greater interest. Did Martin love it? Surely he must. She imagined what it must have been like for him to learn, while still surrounded by the bleak ugliness of prison, that he no longer had any legal claim to the gracious house in which he had grown up. And she thought of what he must feel like now, living here only at the sufferance of his younger brother.

Deep in her thoughts, she did not hear the plod of hooves over the grass bordering the road until the horse and rider were almost beside her. She looked into the rear view mirror and felt an almost panicky embarrassment. Martin!

She started to put the car in gear and then realized that the rider was not Martin, after all.

He stopped beside the car and smiled down at her. "Good afternoon."

"Good afternoon."

"You're interested in my house?"

"It's very beautiful. You say it's yours?"

He dismounted before he answered. He was dark like Martin, but more slender, and perhaps an inch taller. His

142

eyes were gray rather than dark blue, and he looked to be at least five years younger than Martin rather than one. Kate realized that many people would have considered him the better looking of the two men, but he awoke in her none of the interest she had felt at her first sight of Martin, standing on the tide-wet rocks that morning.

"Yes, it's mine. I'm David Donnerly."

"How do you do? I'm Kate Kiligrew."

The name obviously meant nothing to him. He said, still smiling, "You're from up north, of course."

"New York."

"Would you like to see the inside of the house?" He added quickly, as if to assure her that there would be no risk, "After I've shown you the downstairs, my house-keeper will bring us tea. Or a drink, if you prefer."

"That sounds very pleasant."

"Good. Why don't you drive up to the house? I'll tie Commodore to the hitching post and then join you."

She drove up to the veranda, got out. David Donnerly was walking toward her. On the veranda he rang the bell beside the wide, fanlighted door.

It opened. A brown-skinned woman of about fifty, her face calm above the collar of her gray dress, said, "So you're back, Mr. David."

"Yes, and with a visitor. Martha, this is Miss Kiligrew."

The woman gave Kate a pleasant smile and stepped back for them to enter. When they stood in the hall, David Donnerly said, "I'm going to show Miss Kiligrew over the ground floor. In about twenty minutes will you bring us tea on the terrace?" He looked at Kate. "Sure you wouldn't prefer sherry or vodka?"

"Tea will be perfect."

143

Martha left them, walking past the foot of the grace-fully curved staircase toward the rear of the house. David Donnerly led Kate along the row of portraits hanging in the wide, dark-paneled hall. There was a painting of Martin Donnerly, an austere-looking man with a square jaw and with eyes as darkly blue as his elder son's. There was his wife, painted at the age of twenty-five, a nice-looking but not beautiful woman in a bare-shouldered dress of green satin. There were eight ancestral portraits in all, including a Civil War Donnerly in Confederate gray, and the first American Donnerly who had been a "landholder" in his native Ireland, David said. He had sat for his portrait in a white wig and bottlegreen coat and white knee breeches.

At the end of the hall was a closed door. On the wall beside it, hung at right angle to the other portraits, was one of David Donnerly himself, handsome in classic gray flannels and a blue blazer. It had been painted two years ago, he told her.

As David Donnerly showed her the paintings, Kate had been aware of the pride in his voice. She was aware too of how he kept glancing at her, as if eager for her reaction. She had a feeling that it was because of the prospect of enjoying her admiration that he had invited her in. At least she was sure it was not because he found her sexually attractive. She sensed in him none of that gender-awareness which is usually present in even the most casual contacts between men and women.

Perhaps, she reflected, he didn't like girls. After all, he must be past thirty, and evidently still unmarried. If he'd had a wife, surely her portrait too would be on display.

When she had seen all the portraits in the hall, he took her into the drawing room. ("The sofa is Duncan Phyfe. The chairs flanking the fireplace are Chippendale.")

After that they looked through the dining room. ("The dining table is Sheraton. Before the War Between the States, Robert E. Lee twice had dinner at that table.") They went into the library, where another portrait of the first American Donnerly hung above the fireplace. ("Experts say that that is the finest portrait in the house. It's probably a Gilbert Stuart, although we've never been able to authenticate it.")

Suddenly Kate felt she understood his overweening pride in his possessions and his need to use them to impress even strangers. He must have grown up feeling—perhaps with reason—that he, not his brother, was the one who really appreciated this satiny furniture, that Georgian silver on the dining room sideboard. How he must have brooded over the knowledge that Martin was to inherit this house and everything in it. How doubly galling the idea must have been after Martin married Donna Sue Welker, thus making her the prospective mistress of this gracious house.

But one night a blast from a shotgun had changed everything. Donna Sue was dead. Martin, the firstborn and probably the best beloved, was a convicted murderer. And his crushed and embittered father had made his younger son his sole heir. No wonder that these possessions seemed doubly precious to David Donnerly, and no wonder he liked to show them off. Envy and admiration in the faces of others must reinforce his sense of good fortune.

On the red brick rear terrace, Kate and David Donnerly sat on white wrought iron chairs with chintz-covered seat cushions. Pots of azaleas, already in bud, stood on wooden benches. Beyond the terrace stretched a flower garden, some of its beds filled with daffodils and early tulips, others holding rose bushes still wrapped in their winter blankets of straw. Beyond the flower beds stretched more fenced-in pasture land, empty of horses.

The housekeeper brought out a tray which held a teapot, cream pitcher and sugar bowl, a plate of lemon slices, and a larger plate holding little cakes. While they drank tea from cups of flowered pink china, David Donnerly said, "I sold all the horses from that pasture two weeks ago, but next week I'm buying some others. Horse farming isn't the most profitable of enterprises, but it's pleasant."

"I imagine it must be."

"That pasture used to be part of the Donnerly tobacco lands. But when my grandfather inherited the property he sold off most of the land and kept only twelve acres surrounding the house. It hasn't been planted in tobacco for more than fifty years now."

He began to talk of horses again, saying that he planned to start breeding western quarter horses as well as thoroughbreds. Kate felt a growing tension. She had not expected to meet David Donnerly today, nor to be asked into his house. But since she had, surely she should seize the opportunity to ask him about the events of that summer twelve years in the past. Yes, even though her questions would ensure that David Donnerly would tell Martin about her visit.

When he extended the plate of little cakes to her a few moments later, she took one and then said, "You're Martin Donnerly's brother, aren't you?"

Surprise widened his eyes. He set down the plate and then asked coldly, "You know my brother?"

"Yes. I rented the house where he once lived with his wife."

The fact that he apparently hadn't even thought to ask

her where she was staying, Kate reflected, was a measure of his preoccupation with showing off his house and its contents.

"I see. Then perhaps it was with the idea of seeing Martin that you came here today."

Acid in his voice now. Again she thought of the resentment he must have felt all during his growing up years, here in this house to which his brother was heir.

"No. I'd heard that he was in Baltimore, looking at equipment for the boatyard he plans to build."

How tight-fisted of David Donnerly, she thought, to force his brother to go to a bank for a loan. Just that pair of Chippendale chairs in the dining room ought to be worth enough money to buy all the equipment Martin needed.

"Yes, he's in Baltimore. This morning he phoned to say he'll be back tomorrow." He paused and then added, "You seem to know quite a lot about my brother."

"Yes, I've heard a number of things, from various sources." She paused. "Do you think he killed his wife?"

As she had expected, the look on his handsome face said that he found her question in extremely poor taste. After a moment he answered, "Of course I think he did. In spite of the best lawyers my father could hire, the jury found him guilty. And during the years he was in prison, not a shred of evidence to indicate his innocence turned up."

"Did you and your father keep looking for such evidence?"

After a moment he said, his voice colder than ever, "No." He looked at the gold watch strapped to his wrist. "I have business to attend to. And so if you'll excuse me now, I'll see you to your car."

CHAPTER TWENTY-ONE

In front of the house he held the car door open for her and with frigid politeness bade her goodbye. She piloted the VW down the drive and turned toward Mockstown. She felt embarrassment over her curt dismissal, but the emotion was far less strong than her sympathy for Martin. What must he feel like, living in that house on his brother's grudging bounty? Surely he stayed there only because he wanted to save every cent toward his boatyard, that one still-achievable part of the dream he'd had when he was very young, and very much in love, and very determined to succeed in his own eyes and in those of the beautiful creature he had married.

Even though the sun still shone overhead, a ground mist had begun to creep in, an advance guard of the grayish fog bank obscuring the eastern sky. The mist hovered in the hollows of the road that led between the tobacco fields. By the time she turned onto the highway the mist was dense enough that some motorists had switched on their headlights. The thickening fog increased her sense of depression and her unwillingness to return immediately to that silent house.

She would have dinner in Mockstown, she decided, and then go to the movies. The theater there was showing an old Woody Allen picture, she had noticed as she drove through town. "Tonight only," the marquee had said, "*Take the Money and Run.*"

She bought nail polish and cold cream at a drugstore, and then went to the Main Street Café for dinner. Trying to play it as safe as possible, she ordered pot roast. It was quite good. She emerged into the foggy dark and crossed the street to the theater, entering its auditorium just as the credits were coming on the screen.

To her surprise, the place was packed. Because the picture was to be shown only one night, probably almost every Woody Allen fan for miles around had come. She took a second row seat, one of the few available.

She emerged from the theater at nine-thirty, feeling lighter of heart after almost two hours in Woody's woebegone but hilarious company. The fog had grown much thicker. She got into her little car, knowing that on such a night she would practically have to creep over the causeway's bumpy asphalt. Thank heavens that her house was only yards away from the causeway's exit.

It was strange, driving over the fog-bound causeway. For a while hers seemed to be the only car crossing it. She moved as slowly as possible. The fog, like an ever-receding wall in front of her, gave back the diffused glow of her headlights. The sagging iron rail on her side of the road was barely visible, the one on the other side not at all. She could hear but not see the water lapping at the causeway's rocky foundation. Now and then for a few seconds she would hear the voice of the warning buoy offshore from Blackfish Island. It sounded like the lowing of some enormous, lovesick animal.

Another sound, that of a car's engine, a car driven at a faster rate than her own. She looked into the rear view mirror. Nothing at first, then two dim circles of light, rapidly diffusing into a wide glow. The car passed, a large dark shape on her left. For a second or two she could see the red glow of its twin taillights. Then the fog swallowed up not only all sight of the car but all sound of it too. Nothing to hear now but the sound of her car's engine mingling with the wash of water, nothing to see but the slow eddy of fog particles through the headlights' blunted beam.

As she drove, she thought of that hour or a little more in the Donnerly house. After Martin heard of her visit, would he telephone her? Almost certainly. Almost certainly, too, he would sound angry. But she knew he wouldn't be, not entirely. And at least they would be talking to each other—

A burst of light shining into her face.

After a paralyzed instant her foot jammed the brake. The little car bucked. Its engine stalled.

For perhaps six seconds more that light bathed her. Then it disappeared. She heard a car cautiously backing and turning on the narrow roadway, then driving toward the island.

She sat rigid, hands icy on the wheel. Her eyes, glare dazzled moments ago, now saw only darkness.

If she had tried to turn to the right to avoid what seemed an imminent crash, she might have broken through that rusting rail and plunged into at least twenty feet of water. Thank God, though, she had been too startled to even try to avoid a collision. Instead she had just jammed on the brakes and stopped, probably within inches of the other car. It must have been a big car to judge by the height and spacing of its headlamps, a car heavy enough to suffer only minor damage from the impact of a little VW.

Who had the driver been? Some drunk who'd fallen asleep with his car stopped on the wrong side of the causeway? A drunk who had been aroused by the fog-muffled sound of her approaching car? Or had he been driving the car which, back there about half a mile, had passed her own car? She thought of someone who, at some point during the day or evening, had started to trail her. He'd passed her on the causeway, driven close to its end, then turned, parked on the wrong side of the road, and waited until he heard the VW's engine, or saw the glow of its small, low headlamps—

Had he meant to kill her? Her stomach seemed to knot up at the thought. It was nauseating, quite literally, to think that someone feared or hated you enough to try to kill you.

Then she realized that, even though he might have been ready to have her plunge through that railing and drown in her car, he had not been absolutely determined to kill her. If he had been, he would not have driven away. She was alone and helpless on this fog-shrouded causeway. It would have been easy for him to jerk the VW's door open and hit her over the head with a wrench, or even throttle her with his hands.

But he had not, and that must mean that his objective had been to frighten her, frighten her enough that she would go back to New York.

There could be only one reason why someone would be that determined to get rid of her. He was afraid that she would learn the real circumstances of Donna Sue's death.

Unless, she thought, her stomach twisting, Martin really was the killer that others thought him to be, a killer whose twisted malevolence now had fastened upon her—

She wouldn't believe that, not even for a moment.

Her vision had cleared enough so that she could see the mist eddying sluggishly in her headlights' path, see her hands gripping the wheel. Shakily, she put the little car in gear and drove foreward, willing herself to go even more slowly than before, lest again the sudden glare of headlights force her into a collision or into an even more perilous plunge to the water.

She reached the causeway's end. Heart thumping, she drove the last hundred yards along the asphalt road to the dimly looming garage. She did not drive inside. Someone might be waiting in there. Instead she got out of the car and hurried, at risk of stumbling, along the fog-obscured path to the house. She fumbled her key into the backdoor lock, went inside, locked and bolted the door behind her. She moved through the dimness toward the window above the kitchen sink, pulled down its shade. Then she turned on the overhead light.

Thank God she'd had those burglar alarms put in.

Then realization struck her. A wailing alarm might panic a would-be intruder who had not expected such a sound. But it wouldn't frighten someone who, like Chief Bosley, knew that she had installed it. Nor would it deter for long anyone who stopped to think that, in such a tiny community, the alarm would not be connected to police headquarters, or that its clatter probably would not be heard by anyone else on this winter-deserted stretch of beach.

153

Installing the alarms, she realized now, perhaps had not been entirely futile, but almost so. A sense of her own incompetence heightened her fear.

She thought, I've got to call someone. I can't stay here alone, not tonight.

Mrs. Thompson. Maybe she would come.

She went to the cubbyhole under the stairs, switched on the light. After consulting the little pad upon which she had written down a few names and numbers—Mrs. Thompson's, the grocery in Camelot, Leora Kelso's real estate agency—she dialed.

The phone rang five times before Myrtle Thompson answered. Kate said, shakily apologetic, "I hope I didn't wake you."

"You didn't. Sonny and I were just watching the news."

"Mrs. Thompson, could you possibly come here to spend the night, or let me come there?"

The woman said, after a moment, "Better I come there, dear. We don't have much room. But what on earth's happened?"

"Someone—someone tried to run me off the causeway."

"Run you off the causeway! Must have been some drunk. Only a drunk would drive around on a night like this lessen he had to. I'm surprised *you* were out."

"Well, I was. And I'd appreciate it so much if you could spend the night here."

Myrtle Thompson said, after a moment, "I'll be there in about twenty minutes. And if you're really upset, supposing I bring Sonny with me. I'll sleep in that room where you paint and Sonny can have the sofa downstairs. If

154

he drives his truck over, he'll be able to leave for work as soon as he's had breakfast."

"Thank you. Thank you so very much."

Kate moved about the ground floor, drawing the shades. Now that she knew she was not to be alone that night, she felt far less upset. She began to think that maybe it *had* been a drunk on the causeway. It was the sort of crazy thing an extremely drunk man might do, stopping on the wrong side of the road and falling asleep there. More than once she'd read newspaper accounts of drunks driving onto a railroad right of way and passing out there, or even stretching across the tracks before they sank into sodden slumber.

Mrs. Thompson yoo-hooed at the back door. Beside her stood Sonny, a gangling redhead in his middle twenties with a shy grin. Mrs. Thompson bustled around, making up the lower of the two bunk beds for herself and the living room sofa for Sonny.

Even though she was quite calm now, Kate stayed awake long after she began to hear Mrs. Thompson snore gently in the room across the hall. When she finally did fall asleep it was only to come abruptly awake some time later with a sense that several hours had passed.

On impulse she got out of bed and walked to the window. The fog had vanished. The moon—there must have been a second quarter one above the fog, she realized—had set, leaving a dark sky thickly strewn with stars.

She looked down. For some reason she could not define she had expected to see a slender figure down there, upturned face framed in pale straight hair. There was no one.

She turned and went back to bed.

155

CHAPTER
TWENTY-TWO

When Kate came downstairs the next morning she found
Myrtle Thompson seated at the kitchen table with a plate of
scrambled eggs before her. Sonny, the woman said, had
eaten his breakfast and driven off in his truck nearly an
hour ago. Kate put a slice of bread in the toaster, poured
coffee for herself, and then sat down at the table.

As if she felt Kate still needed reassurance, Mrs.
Thompson again asserted her belief that Kate had encountered a drunk the night before on the fog-shrouded
causeway.

"Funniest thing about drunks is the places they pick
to pass out. You've seen Tom Carson? He's the one who
hangs out in front of the liquor store most of the day,
waiting for live ones."

Kate had seen him more than once, a thin figure in
worn navy blue trousers and a ravelled gray sweater, his
fiery red face shaded by a once-elegant yachting cap. Twice
she had seen liquor store customers hand Tom money
before going into the place.

"In the last few years the sexton at the Methodist church has had to cover over the graves he digs the day before a funeral. Otherwise when the mourners show up they're apt to find old Tom asleep down there."

A few minutes later Mrs. Thompson said, "You're sure you feel all right? If you're not, Sonny and I can sleep here again tonight."

"Thank you very much indeed, but I'm over my scare."

With sunlight flooding the kitchen, her panic of the night before had begun to seem a little absurd. After all, nothing bad had happened, not even a scratch on her car.

"Well, see you Friday," Mrs. Thompson said, and left.

Kate looked at her watch. Nine-thirty. Suppose Martin had left Baltimore around eight that morning. He ought to be in Virginia by now. Even if he stopped for a lengthy lunch somewhere, he should be home by mid-afternoon. She imagined him listening to his brother's account of her visit, then striding to the phone or, more likely, driving over here. On the surface, at least, he would be angry. But she still clung to the conviction that underneath he would be glad. Glad that she was still here, even glad that she had felt impelled to drive over to that house where he had grown up.

She washed her breakfast dishes and Mrs. Thompson's, then gathered up the sheets and blankets from the sofa Sonny had occupied and from the lower bunk bed upstairs. She folded the blankets and restored them to their shelf in the hall closet and put the sheets and pillow cases in the bathroom hamper. After that she tried to paint, but all the time she was listening for the ring of the phone.

158

At one-thirty she ate a tuna sandwich lunch without appetite and then returned to her easel. Until almost four she tried to work, then gave it up. She went into her bedroom and, lying on the bed, tried to read Isak Dinesen.

He'd had to stay in Baltimore an extra day, she told herself, or for some reason he had made several stops along the road, and so still hadn't reached the Donnerly house. But all the time she had a growing sense that by now he was at home and had heard about her visit. And contrary to all her wishful imaginings he was thoroughly and coldly angry with her, so angry that he had no intention of coming to see her or even phoning her.

Around five-thirty, unable to bear the silence of the house, she went out to where she had left her car the night before, standing beside the garage. She drove a little way down the asphalt road toward Camelot, then turned into a still narrower one that led to the road encircling the island. When she reached the area where both she and Martin had parked their cars that afternoon they talked on the beach, she drove onto the grass, grass that now had turned spring green.

She descended the steep path to the driftwood log and sat there looking out over the water. She knew now that it was here that she had fallen in love, without realizing it, that afternoon when he told her about the hot summer night twelve years before.

There were two lines of white clouds above the western horizon, their edges so regular that they might have been drawn with a ruler. Already they were turning pink, giving promise of a spectacular sunset. A flock of seabirds wheeled above the water, their bodies black against the rosy glow. She looked at them unseeingly, wondering what she should do. Stay in Camelot at least another week, hoping that something, anything, would cause Martin to change his mind?

The colors in the west brightened, took on an almost tropical splendor. The sinking sun blazed out between the two bands of now red and gold and purple clouds, dazzling her eyes. She felt bleakly aware that she should, but could not, enjoy that brief glory in the west. When you're unhappy beauty brings you, not solace, but added pain.

Besides, if she lingered here she would find herself returning to an already dark house, and that, it seemed to her, would be too much to bear. Abruptly she got up, turned, and began to climb the path up to the bank. After the minutes she had spent staring into that brilliant light she could scarcely see. Near the top of the path she stumbled, pitched forward.

Hands fastened on her shoulders.

Frozen, she stared into the unsmiling face above her own. Martin's face. In that strange light it looked almost blood-red.

Shock hurled her back to that moment on the foggy causeway, when it had occurred to her that it might be Martin in that other car—

She saw shock come into his own eyes. Then a smile, faint and sardonic, lifted his lips at one corner. He released her shoulders, stepped back. Unassisted, one hand grasping the short grass at the cliff's edge to pull herself up, she scrambled to level ground and stood facing him. His blue pickup truck, she saw from the corner of her eye, was parked near the VW.

160

His slight smile was gone now. He said evenly, "Sorry I scared you. You see, I thought you were going to fall."

"I realize that now." Her voice shook. "But for a moment I was so startled that I thought—"

"You weren't just startled. You were scared. You thought that a murderer had grabbed hold of you."

She cried, "That's not true!"

"Oh, come off it!" His voice was harsh. "What you were feeling was plain in your face."

"Martin, listen to me! Try to understand! Something happened last night."

Words tumbling over each other, she told him about those chilling moments on the causeway. She saw the sardonic look on his face give way to alarm.

"You have no idea who it was?"

"No. Myrtle Thompson says it was probably some drunk."

"Maybe so. But if you're smart, you'll assume otherwise. You'll assume it was someone who feels no good will toward you. You'll give up doing damn-fool, self-humiliating things like your visit to my brother's house. You'll pack your bags tonight, or tomorrow at the latest, and go back to New York."

"Martin! Don't you see? If it wasn't just a drunk, it must have been someone who doesn't like my—my interest in you, and in what really happened to your wife. There's someone who's afraid, terribly afraid, of having the truth found out."

He said nothing.

"Martin, don't you yourself want to know who killed your wife?"

161

"Not particularly. It wouldn't bring back those twelve years."

"But it could make all the difference in the world to the years ahead!"

"Kate," he said wearily, "you're not going to find out who used that shotgun. At worst, you're going to put yourself in danger. At best, you're going to prolong something that should never have been started."

"Is that what you really feel? Then why did you stop here when you saw my car? Why didn't you keep driving?"

He said slowly, "I suppose it was because I couldn't resist the chance to see you one more time, even if it was only to urge you to go back where you came from." His voice hardened. "And I'm glad I did stop. The look I saw on your face a few minutes ago clinched it. Things would never work out for us, not in a million years."

"Martin! I told you! I was just—startled."

"Face it, Kate. Last night on the causeway, didn't it cross your mind that I might be the driver of that other car?"

She said nothing.

"Goodbye, Kate." Swiftly he turned, got into the truck. Above the engine's roar he said, "Go back to New York!" He drove over the grass to the road and headed toward Camelot.

Feeling numb, she got into her own car and drove to the house. This time she put her car in the garage before she went into the house by the back door. She walked down the hall, climbed the stairs to the shadowy second floor, and then stopped, frowning.

The door to the linen closet stood open.

Surely she had closed it after she had put away the blankets used by Mrs. Thompson and her son. Yes, she must have closed it, because at least twice that day she had passed that door on her way to the bathroom. She would have noticed if the door had been open, partially blocking her way.

She went to the closet, switched on its overhead light. Nothing seemed different. Blankets on the shelf and, on the floor, the two incongruous stacks of magazines, one of *The New York Review of Books* and the other of *Whispered Confessions*.

She closed the door, shook it to make sure there was nothing wrong with the latch. She went to her room and left her handbag on the dresser. Then, feeling unhappiness like an invisible weight upon her, she descended through the darkening house to the kitchen.

CHAPTER
TWENTY-THREE

Her sleep was broken that night but not with dreams, at least none that she could recall. She would wake abruptly and then lie there, listening. She never heard anything except the clock's tick and the gentle wash of waves. And yet, as she had many times earlier, she had a sense of another presence in the house. Once, unable to resist the impulse, she turned on the bedside lamp. Nothing. No one. Just the curtains she had bought hanging limp at the window. Just her robe lying over a chair back.

She turned out the light and again lay listening. Just that odd silence that gave her the impression of being in a kind of hiatus, as if there had been sounds of stealthy movement before she had begun to listen, and would be again when her attention was elsewhere. After a few moments she went back to sleep.

Waking to hazy sunlight, she put on her robe, went out into the hall.

That closet door stood open.

Something *was* wrong with the latch, then. Well, it soon would be no concern of hers. She had awakened with her decision already formed. Tomorrow she would drive back to New York.

She closed the closet door and went on down the hall to the bathroom.

Over coffee in the kitchen she made her plans. She would telephone Mrs. Thompson and offer her whatever food would be left in the refrigerator and on the cupboard shelves. She would close out her account at the bank. She would see Leora Kelso, settle up about the curtains, and see what part, if any, of her April rent the agent would refund her.

A little after eleven she drove into Camelot. She saw Sonny Thompson's panel truck parked in front of the Bluebell Lunchroom. Tom Carson in his filthy old pants and sweater, and with his yachting cap perched at a debonair angle above his fiery face, sat on the liquor store steps. Kate found a parking place directly in front of the bank and went inside.

Vanessa Weyant sat at her desk inside the railed enclosure. She smiled as Kate came through the little gate.

"Hello, there! And how are you this morning?"

"Fine, thank you," Kate said automatically. She sat down on the straight chair beside the desk. "I've come to close out my account."

"Oh! Sorry to hear that. Are we losing you to one of the banks in Mockstown?"

"No. I'm going back to New York tomorrow."

She saw the leap of gladness in Vanessa Weyant's eyes. So, Kate thought, she had been right. Vanessa wanted to have a clear field with Martin Donnerly. Well, she'd have it

166

now, and maybe she would get him. Kate felt dismayed by the strength of her own anguished jealousy.

Vanessa went away to look up Kate's balance, came back with a check. Both smiling, although Kate found it almost literally painful to smile, they shook hands.

Kate walked to Leora Kelso's office in the shopping mall. When Kate told her she was leaving, the woman voiced a regret that was quite genuine. She had hoped that the New York girl would occupy that lemon, the Hillier house, for months to come. She'd even hoped that she could sell it to her.

Kate said, "Can I get a partial refund on the April rent? After all, I'll be leaving before the middle of the month."

"Oh, no, dear, I couldn't do that." Leora's tone suggested that Kate had proposed something unsavory, if not downright immoral. "But I'll tell you what I will do. Myrtle Thompson tells me that you've kept the place very nice, so I'll refund half your cleaning fee."

"Thank you. About the curtains—"

"Have you got the receipt?"

"Yes." Sure that Leora would ask for it, she had brought it with her.

Leora wrote out a check for half the cleaning fee and half the cost of the curtains. After the usual civilities, they parted.

Kate stepped out into the mall in time to see Chad Garner emerge from the dry cleaning shop. Over one arm he carried a tan raincoat in a transparent plastic bag. At the sight of Kate he smiled and walked toward her.

"How's the painting coming?"

"Not very well." She paused. "I'm going back to New York tomorrow."

He said, after a moment, "I'm sorry. I'll miss you. But then, I thought you'd be leaving soon."

She asked cooly, "What do you mean, you thought I'd be leaving?"

"Don't get sore, Kate. But it was pretty obvious you'd taken a strong personal interest in the Martin Donnerly case."

"So?"

"That could never work out, as I was sure you would realize before long. Whether he's guilty or not guilty, twelve years in prison can do things to a man."

"So he told me," she said, trying to keep the bitter edge out of her voice. Then, changing the subject: "You're still planning to run for Congress?"

"That I am. It's just a matter of raising the money."

"I'm sorry I won't be able to vote for you."

He smiled. "Maybe you will be able to, someday."

She said, after a moment, "You mean, you've thought of running for the Presidency?"

"Why not? I've got a good head of hair, and I could read a speech off a teleprompter as well as the next man. I'll bet you there are tens of thousands of guys with no more qualifications than that who see themselves getting onto the helicopter for Camp David. Why should I be the exception?"

Kate laughed. If she had been going to fall for someone on this little island, she reflected, why couldn't it have been this man with his sense of humor and his refreshingly frank ambition?

She extended her hand. "Goodbye, Chad. All the luck in the world."

When she reached the house she left her car beside the garage and went in the back door.

Instantly she had that sense that someone beside herself was in this house, a sense so strong that the air seemed to vibrate with it. She called, "Mrs. Thompson?" Then, feeling more than a little foolish: "Anyone?"

No sound, but still that sense of vibrancy in the air. She climbed to the second floor. Somehow she had expected to see that linen closet door standing open. It was closed.

She went into her bedroom and laid down her handbag. That feeling of another presence had begun to fade now. But why had it seemed especially strong on this, the last day of her occupancy? Perhaps it was just another manifestation of her inner turmoil, her sense of defeat, her awareness that she would leave Blackfish Island feeling even lonelier than she had when she came here.

After a lunch of canned tomato soup, she went through the sketches and paintings she had done while here, choosing the ones she wanted to keep and carrying the rest out to the trash can beside the garage. She packed her painting gear and nearly all of her clothes. Then, with nothing more to do, she sat on the front step in the watery sunlight and tried to read. But the thought of Martin—in that beautiful old house? driving through Camelot? Conferring with Vanessa Weyant?—kept getting between her and the page.

At last, shortly after five-thirty, she went to the telephone cubbyhole under the stairs. If Martin was having dinner at home, he should be there by now. She would relieve his mind by telling him that she was going back to New York. Even as she dialed, she knew that wasn't her reason for calling. She just couldn't resist the desire to hear his voice for one last time.

She heard the phone at the other end of the line ring twice. Then the housekeeper's pleasant voice said, "Donnerly residence."

"May I speak to Mr. Martin Donnerly?"

"I'm sorry. He isn't here right now."

Was that true? Or had he told the housekeeper, "If a woman calls me, say I'm not here."

The housekeeper asked, "May I take a message?"

Kate felt wretched warmth in her face. "No, thank you." Had the housekeeper recognized her voice? "It wasn't important," she said, and hung up.

She sat there for a moment, hand still on the phone. Wasn't there something else she could do to fill up the time between now and tomorrow morning? Oh, yes, she thought dully. The bed linen in the clothes hamper. She'd put it in a plastic trash bag and place the bag in the trunk of her car. And she might as well take the blankets down from that closet shelf. She climbed the stairs to the upper floor.

The closet door stood open.

She walked to it, switched on the closet's ceiling light. She looked down at the stack of confessions magazines. Probably Donna Sue's, according to Myrtle Thompson. Never before had Kate felt any desire to examine them. Perhaps because they reminded her of Martin's wife she had felt, if anything, a faint repugnance each time she had seen them there on the closet floor. Now, though, obeying some obscure impulse, she bent and lifted the stack into her arms.

In her bedroom she placed them on the floor, sat down on the bed's edge, and opened the magazine at the top of the pile.

The date on the title page was July of twelve years earlier. Almost certainly Donna Sue's magazine, then. Heartbeats quickening, she scanned the table of contents. "Give Me Back My Baby!" "A Fool for His Kisses." "My Husband's Other Wife."

She laid the magazine aside, picked up the next one. It was dated a month earlier. She skimmed the table of contents, then laid the magazine with the first one.

She found the note just inside the cover of the third magazine. It had been written in blue ink on a sheet of pink notepaper. In the upper righthand corner of the sheet a sun-bonneted little girl held a watering can over improbably tall white daisies. The handwriting had an unformed, almost childish look. The note said:

Honey,
Don't come here. I'll meet you next Tuesday, same time, same place. I can hardly wait.

Donna Sue

Kate sat there with the dead girl's note in her hand. Who was this particular Honey, Kate wondered, out of the many men Donna Sue must have addressed in that fashion? Where had she proposed to meet him, and why hadn't she sent the note? Before she could do so, had she and Honey gotten in touch some other way? Small mysteries, probably as unimportant now as they were insoluble.

She replaced the note, laid the magazine aside. She picked up the next one, shook it. Nothing fell out. She had shaken two more magazines before something else fluttered to the floor.

It was a sheet of lined paper, probably torn from a dime-store tablet. It bore a column of words and figures, all in the same childish hand as that note on pink paper. Her gaze swept down the sheet:

Two hundred 100's makes $20,000
Four hundred 50's makes $20,000
Five hundred 20's makes $10,000

A total of fifty thousand dollars, although Donna Sue hadn't written that sum down.

Kate sat rigid, staring at the paper in her hand.

That payroll money, she thought, her heart beginning to hammer. That money in unmarked bills. What was the amount Orren Welker was supposed to have escaped with? Kate could not remember the exact figure, but she was sure it was at least fifty thousand, maybe twice that.

Didn't these figures, in Donna Sue's handwriting, indicate that at least some of that stolen money might have been in her possession? Why else should Donna Sue, the backwoods-born wife of a garage mechanic, have been noting down such large sums?

Kate imagined that girl, with the same perfect face she had seen a few days ago but with a far abler brain, counting that money into piles over and over again, like some young and female Silas Marner—

Where was that money now? Still somewhere in this house? The chances seemed overwhelmingly against that. The police had searched the house thoroughly after Donna Sue's murder. In the years since, scores of people had lived here for a few weeks or months. Surely some of those people—searching for a box of nails, say, in the cellar, or snooping through the attic to relieve the tedium of a rainy day—would long ago have stumbled across those bills if they had still been here.

Nevertheless, wouldn't that column of figures strongly suggest to a court of law that the money had once been in this house? Wouldn't it also indicate that money had been the motive for her murder, rather than her young husband's berserk jealousy? Oh, surely it would.

Should she call Martin? No, not until she had more to go on. In the first place, he might not even come to the phone. In the second place, there was his seemingly unshakable conviction that the whole world, including Kate herself, could never really believe him innocent. Certainly he wouldn't think that a few words and numbers scribbled on a piece of paper could change his future for him. Probably he would tell her, in even harsher terms than before, to stop messing around in his life.

If only she had someone else to turn to. Oh, there was Chief Bosley. But, aside from the repugnance he aroused in her, she doubted his competency in any matter more complicated than a traffic violation.

Still, there was someone. Chad Garner. An able man, and one well acquainted with the payroll robbery. In fact, he himself probably had written the *Clarion* accounts of the robbery and of Orren Welker's death. What was more, Chad Garner liked her. She had been aware of that from the day of their first meeting.

Hurriedly she retrieved the sheet of pink notepaper from that old magazine. Then, with both it and the sheet of lined paper in her hand, she went down the stairs to the telephone.

173

CHAPTER
TWENTY-FOUR

She looked up his number, dialed. When he finally answered after several rings he sounded harassed. "Garner here."

"Chad, it's Kate. Am I interrupting anything?"

"Nothing of world-shaking moment. I'm trying to bake a potato for my dinner. Damn thing won't get done. I think it must be stuffed with cement."

"I'm sorry. I'll call you back later."

"No, wait. Tell me what it is. You sound all worked up."

"I am. Chad, what if I have evidence to show that Donna Sue might have had money from that payroll robbery in her possession?"

He said, after a moment, "Keep talking."

"Mightn't that indicate that someone who knew she had it could have killed her? Some associate of Orren Welker's? Or even the other two Welker brothers? Yes, I know that Martin's lawyer advanced a theory like that at his trial, and that it did no good. But what if I've found some new evidence—"

"Kate, you've got me lost in a bog of speculation. Back up a little ways. What sort of evidence?"

"A list of numbers. It looks as if she sorted the bills into packets of several different denominations and then wrote down the value of each packet. Listen!"

She read the list. "Now couldn't that refer to loot from the payroll robbery?"

"Of course it *could*. But it also might refer to something quite different. And anyway, what makes you so sure that Donna Sue had anything to do with making out that list?"

"It's in her handwriting."

"Now, Kate. You never even knew the girl. So how could you recognize her—"

"The list wasn't all I found. I also found a handwritten note, signed with her name."

She sensed his quickening interest. "What kind of a note?"

"She must have intended it for some man. She addressed him as 'Honey,' and said she would meet him on Tuesday. The point is that the list on the other piece of paper is in the same handwriting."

"All right," he said, after a moment. "Sit tight. Oh, by the way. Have you told Donnerly about this?"

"No."

"Best not to until we can start to figure out what this is all about. If I've read him correctly since he's been out of prison, he won't believe that anything could bring him a new trial. I'll see you in about half an hour."

"But your dinner!"

"I'll open a can of beans," he said, and hung up.

Too excited even to think of her own dinner, she went upstairs and leafed through the rest of the confession magazines. Nothing. Then, very conscious of the two pieces of paper in a pocket of her jeans, she wandered about the lower floor, sometimes stopping to look out a window into the darkness. Again and again she had to fight down the temptation to call Martin.

A car stopping out beside the garage. Footsteps along the path that led past the north side of the house. Evidently he had seen that the living room light was on and had chosen to come to the front door. Its bell pealed.

As she looked at Chad standing on the doorstep in a tweed jacket and unmatching trousers, she saw tense expectancy in his face. That must mean that, in spite of his somewhat discouraging air over the phone, he felt that she might have found something of importance, something that might not only reopen the Donnerly case, but also add luster to his career as a small-town journalist and political candidate.

He followed her into the living room. She reached into her pocket and then handed him Donna Sue's note and her list of computations. He studied them.

"Where did you find these?"

She explained about the magazines.

"You didn't find any more notes?"

"In the magazines? No. I went through all of them, too."

"Did you find notes or letters anywhere else?"

"No, but then I haven't looked. Tomorrow I'll start looking. I'll comb the whole house and the cellar and the attic and the garage. After all, those two papers have been here all these years. Maybe there are others to be found."

"You're not going to New York?"

"New York! of course not. I'm going to stay in this

177

house until I'm quite sure I've learned everything I possibly can about what happened here that night."

"What did Martin say when you told him that?"

"What do you mean?"

"Haven't you called him tonight?"

She said, bewildered, "Why, no. You said it wouldn't do any good. And even before I called you I'd decided it wouldn't."

He put the slips of paper in his left-hand coat pocket. He had lost color, she suddenly noticed, so much so that his hornrims looked very black against his skin.

He said, "Kate, you're an intelligent young woman. How is it that you have been so blindly, stupidly stubborn?"

Uncomprehending, she just looked at him.

He said bitterly, "I tried to prevent something like this from happening. Oh, not that I ever thought you'd get this far. But your hanging around here, your digging into the past, all that was making me—nervous. And so when I saw you in the movies in Mockstown the other night—"

He broke off. She said, after an unbelieving moment, "You were there?"

He nodded. "Toward the back of the house. When the lights came on, and I saw you walking up the aisle, I remembered the fog outside. I thought of how it had probably grown thicker, so thick that you and I were apt to be the only ones crossing the causeway."

Chad Garner behind the wheel of that other car, which to her had been just a pair of blinding headlights. Headlights that could have sent her plunging into many feet of black water.

"I thought you'd leave the very next morning. But you didn't, did you? Instead you kept on and on, and now it's come to this."

178

His right hand went into his coat pocket.

She thought incredulously, why, he must have brought a gun with him. This time he really intends to kill me. In a few seconds I'll be dead, without even knowing why.

Her mind could not believe that, but her body could. Her body was cowering in on itself—stomach knotting, every nerve and muscle contracting—as if to make itself into the smallest possible target.

His hand was coming out of his pocket. She had a sense of remoteness from her shrinking body, as if she had already died.

Then something happened to his face. Behind his glasses his eyes widened, bulged. His jaw dropped.

Evidently he had seen something, something behind her and to her left.

Slowly, slowly, she turned her head and looked over her shoulder. Just for an instant she saw it. The white caftan and the gleam of pale silken hair. Then it was gone, so completely that she could not even be sure that she had seen it. She found herself staring at the wall.

Garner was making inarticulate sounds. She turned toward him. He had begun to back toward the doorway into the hall, both palms held out at arms' length as if to ward something off.

In the doorway he whirled, ran. She heard him jerk open the front door.

After what seemed to her an eternity, but was probably only a few seconds, she found that she could move. She followed him, then halted on the front step. He had fallen, there in the pathway of light that stretched across the rocks to the sand. He was making convulsive movements, as if trying to turn over.

She ran to him and knelt, vaguely aware of the stones' pressure against her knees. She tugged at his shoulder until he lay on his back, one hand clutching his chest, eyes looking up at her with dumb appeal through his still intact glasses.

Oh, God. Any second now he might stop breathing. She couldn't just watch him die. Never mind what terrible thing he had done in the past, or had intended to do tonight. She still couldn't just watch another human being die. If only she had learned CPR. But she hadn't.

Call someone? But who? There was no doctor in Camelot.

Sound of a vehicle stopping out beside the garage. She rose, almost fell as a stone rolled under her foot, and then ran to the side of the house.

She recognized the figure moving toward her. "Martin! Help me! Hurry!"

He broke into a run, halted momentarily at the sight of Chad Garner, then moved swiftly to his side. As Martin knelt, Kate heard the stricken man gasp, "Dr. Clemson!" Then his gaze went vacant, and his breathing seemed to stop.

Kate cried, "Do you know CPR?"

Martin was loosening the man's collar. "Yes. Go in the house and call the Mockstown Hospital. Tell them we're bringing him in. Clemson must be his doctor, so ask them to alert him. And put some blankets in the pickup."

180

CHAPTER
TWENTY-FIVE

Kate could not have said how long it was before the pickup started across the causeway by the light of a half moon low in the west. She rode in the bed of the truck. Blanket wrapped, Chad Garner lay with his head in her lap. She could hear his labored breathing. He was conscious, she knew, or at least had been when Martin, bringing him to the truck in a fireman's lift, had placed him on the blanket-spread truck bed. He had said, "Thanks," and "Dr. Clemson?" and Martin had replied that his doctor had been notified and would be waiting.

When they reached the hospital everything seemed unreal to Kate, like something in a dream or a film White-clad figures hurrying out to the truck with a stretcher. Then the hospital's interior. Bright lights, gurnies whispering over shiny linoleum, a woman's voice on the intercom, calling for a Dr. Snyder.

When they had wheeled Chad Garner away, Kate and Martin sat on a bench in a corridor. After a while Kate asked, "Why did you come to my place tonight?"

"I knew it must have been you who phoned my brother's house and asked to speak to me."

"Then you *were* there."

"Yes. I'd told Martha to say I wasn't. But I kept thinking that maybe something had happened. Maybe you were in some sort of trouble. And so finally—"

He broke off. After that, perhaps because they had so much to say to each other, they said nothing at all.

A tall man in hospital white walked toward them. His face, weary and kind, was topped by coarse gray hair in an old-fashioned crewcut. He said, "Chad wants to make a statement. He wants me to hear it, and both of you, and he wants someone to take it down. I shouldn't allow it. He's very weak. But he's so upset that I feel it will be far less hard on him if I give in rather than refuse."

He added, as if in justification, "It would be different if he were just a patient. But he's a friend, a very good friend."

Martin and Kate followed him down the hall and into a room. Chad Garner in the high bed, an IV line taped to his arm. A monitor behind him on the wall. Its moving line showed a steady pattern of peaks and dips for a few moments, then shot wildly high, steadied itself, then dipped. Near the bed a young nurse stood arranging small bottles and rolls of cotton on a tray.

The doctor indicated a straight chair beside the bed. Kate sat down. She looked at Chad. Then, gaze wincing away from the anguish in his face, she stared at the opposite wall. After a few moments a plump little woman of middle age came in. Dressed in a pink blouse and skirt, she carried a shorthand notebook. She sat down in a chair on the opposite side of the bed.

Dr. Clemson, standing at the foot of the bed beside Martin, said, "All right, Chad."

The man on the bed drew a rasping breath. "I killed her." He turned his head toward the woman with the notebook open on her knee. "Her name was Donna Sue Welker. No, Donna Sue Donnerly."

Dr. Clemson kept a stunned silence for a moment. Then he asked, probably in hope of shortening his friend's ordeal, "Why did you do it, Chad?"

"Blackmailing me." Again he fought for breath. "Letters I wrote her when she was only sixteen and I was over thirty, and married. Fool! Fool!"

He looked at Martin. "Before you even met her. I had no idea she saved them. She married you—how much later?"

"Five years later," Martin said, quietly grim, "when we were both twenty-one."

"Came to me one day. Said she was going to leave you, and needed money—"

The labored voice went on, recounting how he had given her ten thousand in cash. A few weeks later she telephoned him. She wanted fifty thousand more.

His gaze moved to Kate. "Those figures you found. That's how she wanted the money. So many in hundreds, so many in—" He paused, gasping, and then said, "Guess she wrote it down to read over the phone. But I didn't have fifty thousand, not unless I sold stock my father had left me and—and—"

He broke off.

Dr. Clemson said, "And your newspaper."

"Yes. Then no way to—give my wife best care possible. Louise was dying then. You remember?"

Dr. Clemson nodded. "I remember."

"Thought of telling Donna Sue to go to hell. But letters would have—hurt Louise so much. And of course would have finished me forever in politics—"

After a moment the gasping voice went on, telling

that he had promised Donna Sue to bring the money to her house that night. Martin, she had said, would be away overnight, sent out of town by his boss.

Chad had arrived at the appointed time, not with the money but with rubber gloves and a box of shotgun ammunition in his pocket.

"Face all bruised. Said they'd had a fight. Said Martin hadn't left town. Said she'd tried to phone me but I was out. Said, give her the money and get out fast."

He had asked her for a drink of ice water. While she was in the kitchen he put on the rubber gloves and took down Martin's shotgun, handling it carefully so as to blur as few as possible of any fingerprints on the stock and barrel. Swiftly he loaded it. When she came back into the room he had discharged the gun into her face and body from less than ten feet away.

Placing the gun beside her as she lay on the floor, he had begun to search for the letters, terrified that at any moment Martin might return, but knowing that now it was more vital than ever to get the letters out of that house. He had speculated that she might have hidden them in the room she shared with Martin, and that was where he had found them. She had made a slit in the mattress, placed the letters inside, and sewn up the slit.

He'd shoved the letters into his pocket and then, trying to make the crime look like an ordinary burglary, he had gone through the rest of the house, emptying out drawers and turning furniture upside down. Then he had left.

It wasn't until he reached his apartment, where he had lived alone since his wife entered the hospital, that he had discovered that some of the letters he remembered writing to her, some of the most damning, were not there.

"All these years lived in—fear—they might turn up. Must be some place, unless she destroyed them." He looked at Kate. "Then you did find something. List of bills she'd ordered me to bring that night."

He stopped speaking for a moment. On the monitor above his head the moving line peaked, troughed, steadied. He said, "Sure then you wouldn't go to New York. You'd keep looking for answers, maybe go to authorities and demand they search the house again for that payroll money. Instead they might find those missing letters—"

His voice trailed off, then resumed. "I cracked. There's this girl I planned to marry. And I was going to run for—run for—"

Again he fell silent. Then he looked at Martin. "Don't suppose there's anything at all I can say to you."

Martin's voice was hard. "No, better not to say anything at all to me."

With a motion of his hand, Dr. Clemson indicated that Kate and Martin were to leave the room with him. Out in the corridor he said, "We found a revolver in his coat pocket."

Kate had forgotten her impression that Chad Garner had been carrying a gun. She said, in response to the question in his doctor's eyes, "I think he planned to—use it on me."

After a moment Dr. Clemson said, "For the past eight years Chad and I have met once a week at a mutual friend's house to play poker. I thought I knew him about as well as I knew myself. It seems I was wrong."

Kate asked, "Will he live?"

"I don't know. I think he won't, but of course I can't be sure. Good night."

He turned and walked away.

CHAPTER TWENTY-SIX

After an almost silent drive back across the causeway, Martin stopped the pickup beside the garage. He got out, opened the truck's door for her, and she slid down into his arms.

When their kiss ended he still held her close, his hand pressing her cheek against his shoulder. She said, "Do you still want that boatyard?"

"God, no!"

"Why not?"

"I've got you. And soon I'll have an official acknowledgement that I didn't—Why should I want to hang around here in Camelot, with or without a boatyard?"

She drew a little away from him and looked up through the darkness into his face. "Then we'll go to New York?"

"Damn right! And we'll get married, the sooner the better."

She hesitated, not wanting to ask the question that had come into her head, but knowing that she would have to, sooner or later. "But what about those twelve years? You said that they had changed you in ways you could never be rid of."

After a while he said quietly, "I kept thinking of that as I listened to Garner tonight. I hated him so much I could have strangled him as he lay there. Well, maybe prison did that to me, made me into someone who could want to kill an already dying man. Then it hit me that now I didn't have to go on being that sort of person. For the first time since the night Donna Sue died, I was free. Not a convict out on parole, but free as any other man. It was up to me now whether I let those twelve years ruin the next forty or fifty for me."

He paused. "Now come here," he said, and drew her close and kissed her again.

Then she said, looking past his shoulder at the glow of refracted light coming from around the corner of the house, "We left the front door open."

They walked to the front of the house. On the doorstep she turned to look out over the path of light to the waves, frothing as they moved shoreward. He too turned. After a moment he said, "What kept Garner from using that gun?"

She waited several seconds before replying. "It could have been that he felt the attack coming on."

She realized that even though that might be true, it begged the question of why he had suffered the attack. She felt she knew the answer to that. She thought, stomach knotting up, of what she had seen over her shoulder. For her it had been only a glimpse, so brief that it might have been just a trick of her eyesight. But for him, evidently, it had not been brief. He must have been seeing it all the time as he backed across the room, palms held out at arms' length.

But she would never tell Martin about that. After all, he once had loved that girl who had received a shotgun blast in her body and face.

And anyway, she was sure it was gone now, that presence she had sensed from almost her first hours in this old house. There was no need for it to linger.

Looking along that path of light, she thought of the night she had seen the girl down there on the sand. By morning the tide had come in to lap at the rocky part of the beach, obscuring any footprints that might have been left on the sandy strip. But Kate was sure now that even without the erasing tide there would have been no footprints to find. It was not the retarded twin who had walked through the cold moonlight that night.

Martin put his arm around Kate. They turned and walked into the house.